ARLEN CLASSIC LITERATURE

D1612738

THE MILL IN THE NORTH

To Miss L. Lynd

Patricia O'Connor

THE MILL IN THE NORTH

Foreword by Scott Boltwood

ARLEN
HOUSE

The Mill in the North

is published in 2022 by
ARLEN HOUSE
42 Grange Abbey Road
Baldoyle, Dublin D13 A0F3
Ireland
Email: arlenhouse@gmail.com
www.arlenhouse.ie

978–1–85132–289–3, paperback

International distribution by
SYRACUSE UNIVERSITY PRESS
621 Skytop Road, Suite 110
Syracuse, New York
USA 13244–5290
Email: supress@syr.edu
www.syracuseuniversitypress.syr.edu

Typesetting by Arlen House

Digitisation by Siobhán Hutson

Cover artwork:
details from paintings of nineteenth-century mills
by James Arthur O'Connor

Foreword
PATRICIA O'CONNOR:
HER LIFE AND EARLY CAREER

Scott Boltwood

Patricia O'Connor, the pen-name for Norah Ingram, was one of the most widely known and successful Irish woman writers in the decades between Irish independence and the Troubles; indeed, though not as well known today, she was a more prolific and versatile playwright than even Teresa Deevy. Her name frequently appeared in such papers as *The Belfast Telegraph* and *The Irish Times* in various notices marking her surprising artistic productivity: between the publication of her first novel in 1938 and the broadcast of her last short story on Northern Ireland's BBC Home Service in 1961, she authored 2 novels, 5 stories for the radio, and 7 plays for the Belfast stage. Moreover, during the late 1940s and early 1950s, the public would have additionally read of her activities as the President of the Belfast chapter of P.E.N., as well as ordinary member of the Dublin chapter. In fact, *The Irish Times* of 28 April 1951 features a large photo of her, deep in conversation with the writer Maurice Walsh, identifying her as the 'guest of honour' at Dublin's annual P.E.N. Club dinner.

While it is the work of a future project to fully explore her work for the stage, it must suffice now merely to point out that she was one of the most successful and prolific of any Irish playwrights of the era. Her seven plays for The Ulster Group Theatre, Belfast's premier professional theatre from 1940 through 1960, established her as one of the company's three most important playwrights, along with the five plays written for the company by George Shiels and the six by Joseph Tomelty. Indeed, even as early as 1944, on the occasion of her second play, *Voice Out of Rama*, the reviewer for *The Northern Whig* described her as 'one of the most promising of our young dramatists' (*Voice*). Similarly, in 1951, the influential drama critic David Kennedy considered her first among the 'younger writers [who have] emerged from the shadow of the established dramatists, Shiels and Ervine,' in his assessment of Ulster drama in *The Arts in Ulster* (63).

Although throughout her career she would be associated with Northern Ireland, O'Connor was far from a typical Northerner; in fact, she did not even live in the province until accepting a teaching position there in 1930 at the age of twenty-four. Her father Patrick O'Connor was born in Ventry, Co. Kerry, a village on the Dingle Penninsula in 1877, and her mother Annie May Fallon was born in Dundrum, Co. Tipperary, near the border with Co. Limerick in 1880.[1] Patrick joined the Royal Navy in 1895, and until his retirement in 1927, the couple moved to such port cities as Devonport (1901), Cork (1904), Howth (1912), and Peterhead, Abderdeenshire (1918).

O'Connor was born Henrietta Norah O'Connor on 4 December 1905 in a small village called Portnablagh, about two kilometers east of Dunfanaghy, on the north coast of Co. Donegal. Another family relocation allowed her to attend the Church of Ireland boarding school in Celbridge, west of Dublin, when her father was stationed in Howth (Stranney/Ingram 44). Following their move to Scotland, she started at Dunfermline High School in 1920 and, in her article 'Choosing Teaching as a Career' (1944), she admits, 'I did not choose teaching as a career. I was conscripted' (92). In other words, since there were few other careers open to women, she rather passively followed it, eventually earning her teaching certificate in 1928 from Dalry House, a Teacher Training College in Edinburgh affiliated with the Episcopal Church.

O'Connor started her career as Principle Teacher at the Viscount Bangor National School in Killough, a coastal town southeast of Downpatrick, Co. Down, in September 1930. Her elder sister Teresa had taught there since 1926; when she accepted a position as Vice Principal at Portadown High School, O'Connor accepted her sister's position as Principal Teacher at Viscount Bangor, teaching academic subjects – primarily English, Maths, History, and Geography – as well as Singing, Drawing, and Physical Training. She worked in this two-room school of approximately thirty students until 1945, when tuberculosis forced her to retire. In February 1933, she married William 'Rex' Ingram, becoming Norah Ingram, in Bovevagh Parish Church, Co. Londonderry, and they remained married until her death in February 1983.

With *The Mill in the North*, we return to O'Connor's emergence as a writer in early 1938, four years before the staging of her first play. Although her other – and last – novel, *Mary Doherty*, was also to appear that year, we know that *The Mill in the North* is her first largely because its publication was advertised in the *Irish Times* of 4 June 1938, six full months before the announcement for *Mary Doherty* on 3 December. Proof that the novel remained popular in the Republic is evidenced by the fact that it was listed in the 'What Dublin is Reading' section of *The Irish Times* on 10 September 1938, three months after its publication.

Fortunately, several of O'Connor's letters to Major-General Hugh Montgomery, written in the latter half of 1937, are preserved in Montgomery's archive housed in Belfast's Public Records Office (PRONI). In these letters, we find the young, aspiring author engaging the elder statesman in a spirited and wide-ranging discussion of politics and politicians on both sides of the Irish border. O'Connor seems to have initiated the correspondence because of her interest in Montgomery's 'Ulster and the Empire,' a short opinion piece published in the Summer 1937 edition of *The New Northman*, a Queen's University journal. In it, he argues that the British Empire's military security and relations with other Commonwealth nations would be greatly enhanced through the achievement of 'some workable form of partnership between North and South' (37).

O'Connor seems to have initiated the correspondence in mid 1937 to encourage Montgomery to form 'a non-sectarian United Ireland Party' (16 June 1937). Indeed, she argued that such a party, if willing to set aside sectarianism, would win support from Protestants and Catholics, if it focused on economic development, what she called 'a definite, reasonable business proposition.' In a later letter, she sought to convince him that an individual with his prestige could convincingly make the argument for 'Irish unity, from an Ulster point of view' (12 October 1937). Through such comments O'Connor reveals herself to be, like Montgomery, an Irish Protestant who believes in a united Ireland: 'The border was the most insane bit of procrastination ever conceived – even in the mind of a Conservative Politician.' Even though she confides to Montgomery that she had 'no patience for Mr De Valera's supposed Republican ideas,' her letters are filled with powerful sympathy for the Irish state; indeed, she even mentions to Montgomery that *The Belfast News-Letter* had published one of her letters to the editor that she had signed merely as 'A Southerner.'

We are fortunate to have this correspondence because most of it dates to the year leading up to the publication of *The Mill in the North*, and O'Connor freely comments on the challenges she faced as a writer working in a politicised milieu. In referring to a play submitted to the Abbey, O'Connor summarizes her writing strategy in a letter dated 12 October 1937:

> Propaganda that offends is worse than useless; on the other hand undue timidity achieves nothing. It is not always easy to hit the middle course, which will be the only solution to Ireland's problems.

She additionally explains that in *The Mill in the North* she endeavoured to limit the novel's politics to the 'under current' that pervades the background. However, she recognises that the politics of Northern Ireland must occasionally break through to the surface, to become the novel's subject defining her characters. In a later letter, dated 29 December 1937, she discusses one such example that her publisher attempted to suppress. She reveals that though she was an as-yet unpublished, unknown writer, she refused to alter her work because of her publisher's political timidity:

> I used the expression: 'Nancy Montgomery had been brought up to obey her parents, love God and honour the King.' When the first proofs came back, the 'honour the King' had been deleted. I promptly put it back in. In the second proofs it was deleted again. I inserted it once more. In the last proofs it was left in and there was a note from the Editor: 'It is too expensive to continue this argument – have it your own way!' They had to reprint the whole galley twice over the position of the King.

Although she jokes to Montgomery that 'The Talbot Press regard me as a black, bigotted [sic] Unionist!' her letters reveal that she was painfully aware of the challenges faced by Northern writers seeking publishers in the South.

With the publication of her second novel *Mary Doherty*, which her publisher Sands of London claimed 'deals straightforwardly with the mixed marriage problem' O'Connor seems to have confirmed her Dublin publisher's claim that she was a novelist 'of outstanding ability.' She continued to write fiction, in the form of short stories, throughout her career; her first, 'Silk Stockings' was broadcast on Radio Éireann in November 1938, while the last was broadcast on the BBC Northern Ireland Home Service in October 1961. Moreover, she seems to have retained her skill as a writer of prose despite her career focus on drama: her story 'A Parable in Reverse' won the 1959 BBC Short Story competition.

Perhaps her penchant for the story suggests why she ultimately preferred writing for an audience to writing for readers: rather than publishing her stories in more conventional venues, like *The Bell* or *Lagan* (where, incidentally, she published essays), all of O'Connor's stories were written for broadcast. Thus, these stories shared with her plays both the immediacy of performance, and the embodiment of her characters by actors. Ultimately, both O'Connor and Deevy found that the Abbey Theatre management of the late 1930s had no interest in staging works by women (Bank xii). Deevy found a place for a few of her late works with Radio Éireann. Conversely, O'Connor was fortunate that the Ulster Group Theatre opened as a year-round, professional theatre in 1940, and by December 1941 it had staged its first original play, Jack Loudan's *Story for Today* about the Belfast Blitz. O'Connor's first play, *Highly Efficient*, about the friendship between Catholic and Protestant school mistresses, would premiere soon afterwards, on 21 September 1942, inaugurating a career as playwright that would make her known throughout Ireland.

WORKS CITED

Bank, Jonathan, *et al.*, *Teresa Deevy Reclaimed: Volume 1* (New York, Mint Theater Co., 2011).

Kennedy, David. 'The Drama in Ulster' in Sam Hanna Bell, John Hewitt and Nesca Robb (eds), *The Arts in Ulster: A Symposium* (London, George G. Harrap, 1951), 47–68.

Montgomery, Major-General Hugh, 'Ulster and the Empire,' *The New Northman* v. 2 (Summer 1937), 36–37.

O'Connor, Patricia, 'Choosing Teaching as a Career,' *Lagan* 2 (1944), 92–96.

'Irish History' (Letter to the Editor), *The Belfast News-Letter*, 28 February 1940, p. 8.

Letters to Major-General Hugh Maude de Fellenberg Montgomery, C.B., C.M.G. of Blessingbourne, Public Records Office of Northern Ireland (PRONI), D2661/C/1/I/1–12.

Stranney, William and Valerie Ingram, 'Patricia O'Connor, Killough Playwright,' *Lecale Review* 13 (2015), 42–50.

'*Voice out of Rama* at Group' (Review), *The Northern Whig & Belfast Post*, 6 September 1944, p. 3.

PATRICIA O'CONNOR'S WORKS

Radio Stories

'Silk Stockings', 15 November 1938, Radio Éireann.

'More Excellent than His Neighbour', 15 June 1956, BBC Northern Ireland Service.

'The God Out of the Machine', 22 October 1958, BBC NI Service.

'Jack of Hearts', 10 November 1961, BBC NI Service.

'A Parable in Reverse'

Other Works

'Choosing Teaching as a Profession', *Lagan* 2 (1944), 92–96.

'Coloured Balloons' (Editorial), *The Bell* XV 5 (1948), 57–58.

'Canvassing Disqualifies' an unstaged, one-act play published in *Four New One-Act Plays* (Quota, 1948).

NOTE

The biographical details in this paragraph are taken from Stranney and Ingram's 2015 article 'Patricia O'Connor, Killough Playwright.'

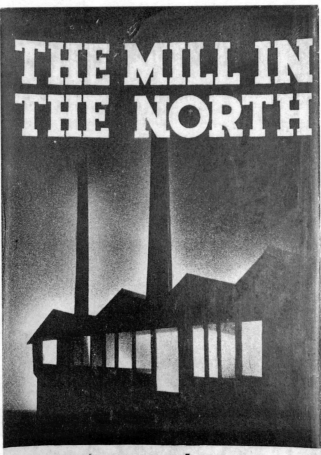

front cover of hardback and paperback editions of
The Mill in the North
(Talbot Press, 1938)

THE MILL IN THE NORTH

CHAPTER ONE

The Annual Meeting of Harkness, Harkness and Harkness Limited was over. The same old story; linen had slumped, was slumping, and looked like continuing to slump. But the firm of Harkness, Harkness and Harkness could stand any amount of slumps. There was a good deal to be said in favour of capital when it came to the aid of a business on the down grade. It acted as a reassuring brake, which made all the difference in getting round tight corners. The Harkness bank balance had certainly enabled the Ringawoody Spinning Mill to be steered safely round a corner, which had brought half the linen mills in Ulster to a dead stop – not to say a bad smash.

John Harkness shook hands with Mr Davidson, his capable clerk and secretary. 'I must compliment you on the way you keep your books, Davidson,' he said briskly. He had made this remark regularly every year for some fifteen years. The words were almost part of the Meeting's routine.

William Davidson bowed gravely. 'Thank you, Mr Harkness. I appreciate that very much.' His reply was also more or less invariable. Though in his younger days he had said, 'I am glad that I give satisfaction, Mr Harkness.' But with the passing of the years and more mature reflection he had decided that the first formula rather inclined to repeat the compliment already paid him by Mr Harkness. After careful consideration he had therefore altered it to the one he now employed.

At this stage, Mr Harkness sometimes asked about Mrs Davidson and the family. Today, however, he did not do so, but turned instead to old Mr Seed, the mill manager. William Davidson was dismissed. He bowed again with even greater gravity to the room in general and withdrew unobtrusively.

The two elderly men there shook hands more warmly. John Harkness's social sense was curiously intermingled with a regard for long and loyal service. Davidson was a splendid servant. Mr Seed was almost an equal.

'How is the lumbago, Tom? I must say you stand the years well,' he said heartily.

Thomas Seed shook his head. 'Not so good, Mr Harkness, not so good. The truth of the matter is, I am not a young man. Not by forty years.'

John Harkness laughed. 'Now, Tom, I cannot let you say that. You know you have not many years ahead of me. But let me hear anyone saying I am an old man. Just let me hear them!'

The manager laughed at such a ridiculous idea. John Harkness could rest assured that he would never hear anyone saying anything of which he did not personally approve. Not in the Ringawoody Spinning Mill at any rate. He was not the kind of man on whom one tried the new freedom of speech movement or any other nonsense of that type.

Thomas Seed, having laughed to order, instantly became serious again. 'We must think of the mill, Mr Harkness. This past year took a good deal out of me. I do not want to hold a position that is getting beyond me. The time is fast approaching when you will require another man. I feel it is my duty to draw your attention to the fact.'

John Harkness frowned. 'I dislike changes, Tom, but I suppose you are right. What about Davidson? I suppose he is pretty sound? Ought to know the ropes too?'

Thomas Seed considered the matter thoughtfully. 'I do not think you could make a better choice, Mr Harkness. I would venture to say that Mr Davidson is your man. He has everything to recommend him. He deserves it too after his many years of service. It would be much more suitable than bringing in a manager from one of the closed mills.'

John Harkness was in complete agreement. 'Certainly, certainly. I would not think of such a procedure. I like to train my own men. Well ... that is settled. But I hope that it will not be necessary to make any change for some time.'

Thomas Seed hesitated. For many years he had had to keep reminding Mr Harkness of certain details with regard to the staff, but he still approached the task with diffidence. 'It will be necessary to take on a boy for the office, Mr Harkness. Somebody who will be able to take over Mr Davidson's work later. He will need some training. I think you ought to give the matter your attention.'

John Harkness frowned again. 'Of course. I shall see about it at once. Do not let me forget. I think that is all. No complaints?'

'No, Mr Harkness, everything is going very smoothly ... I dismissed the Montgomery girl for swearing ... She was an excellent spinner. It was most unfortunate.'

'Yes, yes,' said John Harkness testily, 'but rules must be observed, Tom. Has she been looking for her job again?'

'Yes, Mr Harkness. She wanted to speak to you before the Meeting. I told her that was impossible, but I gave her permission to wait. I think you ought to see her, Mr Harkness. She is usually very well behaved and there is a big family. I say this because I know you take everything into consideration, and personally, I should like to give her another chance.'

John Harkness grunted. 'Very well, I'll see her. But discipline is discipline, Tom. You remember the set of impudent chits we had to handle when we started? I tell you frankly I am not disposed to make exceptions. It leads to trouble.'

Thomas Seed ventured no further. 'Whatever you think, Mr Harkness. I shall tell the girl to wait in my office. Good afternoon, Mr Harkness; Good afternoon, Mr Edward; Good afternoon, Mr Charles,' and, bowing gravely, if a little stiffly, to Harkness, Harkness and Harkness, the mill manager withdrew.

John Harkness turned to his sons. 'Old Tom is finished. He is getting soft-hearted – a sure sign. I am sorry. We shall have to give him a decent pension.'

'I should say so,' said Charles, the younger son, a mere child in his early thirties. 'Mr Seed is a fine old codger. But, father, I don't like this dismissing a girl for swearing. Did she actually swear at any of the executive committee?'

'Charles!' said his father. 'When I want your opinion I am still capable of asking for it.'

Charles Harkness was very much his mother's son. In her young days the late Mrs John Harkness had been inclined to be what her devoted husband described in others as 'an impudent chit' which probably accounted for the sincere affection and admiration which her husband accorded her to the hour of her death. Aye, and would continue to accord until the hour of his own. Charles Harkness was not appreciably disturbed by his father's rebuke. He grinned cheerfully and turned for support to his brother. 'Well, Edward, let's have a few carefully chosen words from you. I seem to have put it badly.'

Edward Harkness shook his head. 'Sorry, Charles, I'm afraid I cannot support your chivalrous schemes. Business and sentiment make a bad combination.'

'Sentiment be damned!' said Charles. 'It's a case for ordinary humanity. Even old Seed is in favour of clemency; the average director would leave a case like this to the discretion of the manager.'

John Harkness buttoned his overcoat with an air of finality. 'At the present time, the average mill director is having an excellent object lesson on the disadvantages of being average. Harknesses were never average. They never will be average, not while I am alive. You may be too young to appreciate the value of discipline, but it has a value, Charles, in real hard cash. You two need not wait for me. I have a number of things to see to.'

When the old man had gone Charles turned to his brother with a little smile. 'The spirit of the North!' he said. 'Was the captain of the Bounty an Ulsterman?'

Edward Harkness did not smile. 'I should not say so. The captain of the Bounty mixed his admiration for discipline with dishonesty, which accounts for the mutiny.'

'Maybe,' mused Charles, 'but there are times when Harkness, Harkness and Harkness give me a pain in the neck.'

Nancy Montgomery had waited for her interview with Mr John Harkness for over two hours. Long before the waiting period had elapsed she was earnestly praying that there would be no interview. In obedience to her mother's orders she had ventured to ask Mr Seed for another chance. At no time had she been prepared for an interview with the awe-inspiring man who owned the mill. As far as she was capable of fearing anything, Nancy Montgomery feared the name of Harkness. She had been brought up by a well-meaning mother in the fear and respect of the Almighty – and Harkness, Harkness and Harkness.

Nancy Montgomery was twenty years of age and looked thirty. At fifteen, when she had been first taken into the mill, she looked twelve. For two years she continued to look a rather tired child, after which she looked what circumstances had made her, a youngish woman whose first bloom had faded.

Nancy's appearance would probably be dismissed with the one discourteous, infinitely-unjust adjective – 'common' by the ordinary middle-class individual. She had dressed up for her big effort. She wore a tweed coat featuring the new, large, gay check, as now worn by the smarter set. At least that was how the catalogue described it, and Nancy continued to accept the evidence of the printed word rather than that of her own eyes. The coat had been stocked in two sizes, neither of which had been Nancy's. She would have been wiser had she taken her mother's advice and ordered the larger size, but at twenty one naturally shrinks from the matronly insinuation of the word 'outsize'. The coat was the most important, but, unfortunately, not the most conspicuous article of her attire. She wore a small red hat. Bright red suited Nancy because she was very dark, and Nancy took the advice of the 'Woman's Page' and analysed her appearance before buying her clothes, especially her Sunday ones. She had a pink satin blouse the shine of which matched the highlights of her artificial silk stockings, and a pair of high-heeled, patent leather shoes, which, although quite new, had already begun to crack despite all guarantees to the contrary. Nancy was not seriously disappointed. She had not altogether believed the shop girl's assurance. It had not been printed, and, as Nancy cheerfully explained, you cannot expect to get the best patent leather at 'six-and-eleven.'

Though built on a generous scale, Nancy Montgomery was not ungainly, and despite her carefully-selected wardrobe, she was a fine-looking young woman. A very little discrimination on the part of the observer would have revealed her as an attractive and handsome girl. Even as it was, she was striking, perhaps a little too striking.

A woman with the wisdom of twenty who looks thirty is hardly calculated to be a success in a court of private appeal. When in addition, she affects a red hat and a pink blouse, and her judge is an elderly, conservative gentleman, with his own fixed views on most things, her case is indeed hopeless.

Nancy was nervous. Nerves loosen the cords of caution and make for indiscretion. When John Harkness entered the office, she instantly sprang to her feet and burst into a torrent of angry, excited, incoherent speech. John Harkness looked her over with a complete lack of sympathy; as soon as she had finished, he sat down at Mr Seed's desk and proceeded to examine some books. When he found what he was looking for he took a pad and carefully wrote down some particulars. Then he turned to Nancy Montgomery. 'Stand over here, please.' (He indicated a spot in front of the desk). 'Your name, is, I believe, Anna Montgomery? You have been employed here for five years. You were dismissed for using bad language while at work. Are these particulars correct?'

Nancy knew that she was being snubbed. 'Yes,' she said sullenly, deliberately omitting the 'sir.'

'Well?' said John Harkness. 'What have you to say? And will you please speak slowly.'

Nancy's knowledge of men was limited to the reactions of the village lads to her direct, if over-hearty wit, but she had a shrewd idea that she need expect little in the way of mercy from a man who looked at her in the manner that John Harkness adopted. Well, what the hell did she care? Let him go to the devil with his old mill. Nancy's temper saved her from unavailing humiliation. Without its strengthening warmth she might have remembered her mother's laments, or the fact that she was saving up for a dance frock, and pleaded for her lost job.

'I know rightly it's no good. I'm not for saying anything,' she muttered.

John Harkness frowned. 'May I ask then why you asked for an interview?'

'I never asked for no interview with you. 'Twas Mr Seed I asked about my job. He said as I was to see you. But what do you care? Nothing, you don't.'

'You are very insolent. Were I prepared to reconsider your case, your attitude would not help you.' John Harkness was angry. Otherwise he would have ordered the girl from the room.

'Didn't I just know you weren't going to reconsider nothing? I'm sacked, and you'll see I stay like that. Well, you aren't my boss anymore and I'll say what I damn well like. Insolent, indeed? Did God Almighty give anybody orders to crawl on their hands and knees to you? No fear, He didn't. My mother is a widow, and there's six of us at home now without a job among us.'

'I am afraid that does not concern me.' The man's voice was harsh. In his heart he knew that such a case did concern him.

'No. Nothing concerns you if it doesn't suit you to hear. But you can concern yourself over me saying a curse word when I got the hand nearly took off me in your old machine. I always did my work right, and worked hard. You never gave me anything for nothing. I earned my pay and earned it hard. You can keep your job and your nice quiet girls, what'll take good care they won't get no reason to curse, for they wouldn't put a hand to it if all the yarn in Ringawoody tangled. I saved you about five quid.' (She held out a scarred hand). 'Look at all I got for my trouble, and because I said "Damn" I lose my job. That's justice, is it?'

John Harkness rather wished that he had heard all the facts from Seed before he began the interview. But it was now too late to do anything. The girl had gone too far. 'I am sorry your hand was hurt. The firm will make you some recompense with respect to your injury. Had you explained the matter in a proper manner, I should have been inclined to take a more lenient view of your offence. As it is I could not possibly keep you, even if I wished to do so.'

Nancy tossed her head. 'Wait till you're asked! I'll live without your job, don't you fret, and you can keep your compensation. I don't want no money from you. My hand isn't all that badly hurt. I didn't come to beg. I came to ask for my job. Now I don't want it. But as there's a God in Heaven you'll be punished yet. I never wished anyone harm before, but I won't shed no tears when you get what's coming to you. No fear I won't! I'm only sorry that I can't give a hand.'

John Harkness rose. He was no longer angry. The girl's spirit and her disdain of charity pleased him. He had given her an opening and she might have tried to make the most of her injury. 'We are wasting time. You may apply to me for a reference if you require one. I am perfectly satisfied that you were an excellent and useful worker. I am sorry this has happened. We cannot afford to lose such workers.'

His tone silenced Nancy completely. She turned to the door.

'Just a moment!' As he spoke, John Harkness knew that he was being unwise. He was permitting a personal consideration to impinge on a business transaction. 'If you have a sister we would consider her application for your job.'

Nancy shook her head. 'Thank you, sir. My sisters are still at the school.'

'Well, perhaps, later on. That is all, you may go.'

Nancy had a two-mile walk after her unsuccessful mission. The Montgomerys had been obliged to leave the mill house in Ringawoody when Nancy lost her job, and had installed themselves in a labourer's cottage on the Ballynahinch road.

Nancy wished that she had worn her working shoes as she tackled the long tramp with glum patience. She realised that she had been a fool. She might have had a chance if she had shown a little common sense. Well, it couldn't be helped now. Like as not it wouldn't have made a whit of difference, and she'd liked fine telling the old devil something. If the worst came to the worst she'd get a job in service. The pay was bad for the likes of her that could earn over her pound a week at the spinning, but she'd get her food and her keep and the dance frock could wait a bit. Fashions changed that quick that by next year she'd be right pleased she hadn't bought one this year, and, maybe, after all, she would not get an invitation to the Farmers' Dance. 'Twas only an odd mill girl as ever was invited, and Frank Orr had not looked her way for many a day. 'Twas said in Ballynahinch his father was making a match for him with one of the Stewart girls from the Moate. Yon white-faced Lizzie one, more than likely. She'd need all her dowry to make up for yon skinny face of hers. But the Stewarts had a right good farm, and, though the Orrs were said to have plenty themselves, farming folk looked for a bit of money with the bride. Aye, they could stick to their grand notions of dowries and devil a bit Nancy Montgomery cared for all the Frank Orrs in Ulster. Not that she wouldn't do right well on a farm. She'd look for a job like that where they kept a girl for the outdoor jobs. The best of being in service was you didn't have to stand no bossing. The mistress had to keep a civil tongue in her head or you could always walk out and pick up another job in no time. Good servants were scarce, and Nancy could work beside anyone in the house – even a County Down farmer's wife. She was well rid of the mill.

When she reached the cottage, however, she was less cheerful. Her mother would be disappointed, and when Mrs Montgomery was disappointed she was inclined to make impartial attacks on anyone within reach. With the winter coming on, the three little girls still at school, and the boy Peter, who was considered too clever to be wasted on labouring and who was evidently not sufficiently clever to find himself any more high class employment, out of work, the prospect far from bright. The widow's pension made no provision for grownup children who lost jobs or were unable to find them.

Nancy slipped quietly into the kitchen prepared to face the impending storm with the small stock of patience she possessed. The kitchen table was set for one, and Bessie, the eldest of the school girls – a small, freckled, red-haired child of thirteen – was carefully watching a kettle on a more than usually robust fire.

Nancy looked her pleased surprise. 'Did you keep tea for me? That's fine. I'm right hungry.'

'Ma said as I was to stay in to get your tea,' said the child with an air of mystery. 'And you are to get a boiled egg to your tea and toast. I'll make the toast now, and you can keep your eye on the clock for the egg.'

Nancy threw off her coat. The magnitude of her amazement might be measured by the fact that she tossed her Sunday coat on a chair instead of hanging it up with the care and ritual to which a Sunday coat is entitled. 'Is this a wake?' she demanded. 'See here, Bessie, just you tell me what's happened or I'll warm your ear.'

Bessie cut two slices of bread and carefully placed one at the end of a fork. 'Honest, Nancy, I don't know. Davy John Orr was in when I came home from the school. Him and ma were having tea, and they had some of the cake from last Christmas, and that wee tin of biscuits that was never opened – there's eleven left.'

'Shut up about the biscuits. What did Davy John Orr come for?' said Nancy impatiently.

'That, I don't know. Ma sent me out to play. Half-an-hour ago she called me in. She said as I was to get your tea and to go to Moore's for three eggs and as you was to get an egg, so she did.'

'Where did ma go?'

'To Ballynahinch. She won't be long now. She says she'd be back on the bus.'

'Glory be to God!' said Nancy. 'Someone has left us a fortune. Is that egg done?'

'Did you no watch the clock?' asked Bessie, placidly. 'How would I be knowing? Here, the toast is ready. I'll wet the tea and you can lift the top off the egg and see if it's right.' She busied herself with the careful measuring of the tea and Nancy lifted the egg. 'Is it all right?' asked the small child with polite fussiness.

'Grand!' said Nancy.

Bessie poured out the tea with an air of housewifely pride. 'Do you like that tea now?' she asked anxiously.

'I couldn't have made it better myself. Now sit you down. I want to hear more of this fortune.'

Bessie sat down obediently, folding her hands primly on her lap. 'There's something going on,' she said. 'But what it is I couldn't say. Ma was terribly pleased.'

'Did she not give you a hint at all?'

'She did not. She said she was to see some friends in the town, and she was going to ask at the Post Office to get the pension money early, for she had some shopping to do.'

'It's a fortune! Nothing less than a fortune would make ma go into debt for a day. I wonder how much it is and who 'twas that left it?'

Bessie considered the matter earnestly. 'Do you think she will get me new shoes?'

Nancy finished her egg with a flourish and skilfully shied the shell on the fire. 'Of course she will, Bessie. New shoes, new stockings, new dresses – we won't know ourselves. We'll be sending you to the new High School in Downpatrick. You'll be talking with an accent none of us will be able to make head or tail of, and strange languages, Bessie, French and German and God knows what! My, but you are the lucky girl, Bessie! I wish the money had come in time to give me a grand education.'

'I'm no good at the school,' said Bessie doubtfully.

'Talk sense, girl,' said her sister sharply. 'Look at the grand match you could make with a fine education. You could pick your choice from all the farmers' sons in the country. I wish I'd had the chance.'

Bessie was less cheerful. 'Maybe there's no fortune at all.'

Nancy emptied her mouth hastily with more attention to speed than hygiene. 'Of course there's a fortune. What else could it be? My, but you're quare and dumb! It wouldn't be me but I'd have heard all the crack.'

Bessie sprang to her feet eagerly. 'Here's ma! My, but I'm nervous. Is there any tea there for her?'

She rushed wildly to open the door. 'Ma! ma! Nancy is back. I made her tea just as you said. What's in the basket? Can I take the things out?'

Mrs Montgomery swept into the room. She was a small woman of about forty with dark curly hair and very bright eyes that gleamed now with pride and triumph. Her cheeks were flushed. She was quivering with excitement and information. In her moment of exultation she looked younger almost than her eldest daughter. 'Let be, Bessie, and sit down. I'll take a cup of tea if there's one left. Nay, Bessie, add no water, I'll take it strong. Nancy, I have news for you.'

Nancy was excited also. 'What is it at all, ma? Is there money left us?'

Mrs Montgomery sipped her tea slowly. 'There is no money for us, but for you there's money, a grand house, and a husband.' She sounded like an old spaewife telling a fortune.

A husband!' said Nancy in amazement. 'Did Davy John Orr come to make a match for ...?'

'For you and Frank? He did. Never was I so taken on the hop in this mortal life. Not a drop of anything in the house ... It was a mercy to the Lord I kept that wee bit of cake and them biscuits. You know, Nancy, there's such a thing as second sight. I had a feeling about them biscuits. Many's the time I was tempted to open them when yon clipe of a woman Moore was in, just to let her see we were doing fine, but no ... I thought to myself ... I'll have more need of them another time. Now was I right?'

'You were right, ma,' said Nancy. 'But tell me what he said. Was there no word of a match between Frank and Lizzie Stewart?'

Mrs Montgomery drank more tea before replying. 'Yon one!' she said contemptuously. 'Aye, there was word of it. Frank was never for marrying her but between ourselves, Davy John is grasping. A fine straight man, but grasping. He had the notion that there would be a grand dowry with Lizzie ...'

'And was there no?' demanded Nancy.

'Nay. Not what the old miser expected; and that led to the fighting and gave yourself the chance, lassie. Lizzie herself is no fool, mind you, and that mother of hers could drown eels in a dry sheugh, but the old man wouldn't leave it to the womenfolk. The men, aye, think they can fix things. The upshot of it all was the two old fellows were at it something terrible. Davy John said that Lizzie's face had been in the family that long it was mouldy, and she was known as the laziest trollop in the Six Counties. And old Stewart nearly riz the roof with the yelps of him. He said that Davy John had the whole farm mortgaged to the bank; mind you, that's a damn lie, Nancy, as I made it my business to find out – and that he was looking for money to keep the roof over his head, no for a decent wife for his son. That was the best thing he said, Nancy, for Davy John ups and says that he would show the liar he was and Frank would have the fine, hard-working girl he wanted though she had no a penny to her. Did you ever hear the like of it, Nancy?'

'I did not. Maybe he'll change his mind when he gets back his senses.'

'Maybe he will, and I wouldn't doubt it, if I know Davy John. But it will be no easy matter for him to get clear of me, I'm telling you. Leave it to your ma. Davy John has asked me for you for Frank, and after thinking the matter over I consented. 'Twould take a smarter man than Davy John to get out of it now, besides young Frank is all on for it. I believe yon lad's in love with you, Nancy.'

Nancy blushed. 'Quit your nonsense. Sure I haven't spoken to him for over a month.'

Mrs Montgomery helped herself to more tea. 'That was Davy John's work. But you ought to be the quare grateful girl this day both to your mother and the good Lord. If I hadn't brought you up decent and kept you in from trapesing the roads all hours, like some of them hussies in the mill, do you think the likes of Frank Orr would look at you? Nay, nay. I did my duty by all my children and signs by I reap my reward. I walked into Mrs Moore's, and says, "Davy John Orr was in this afternoon asking for Nancy for his Frank. It's no a great match, but it's well to get them married anywhere these days." You could have counted her teeth. Frank is to get the Ballycam farm, and you'll live there. Three thousand pounds they paid for it. Davy John told me four, but that was a lie. But it's a grand farm and a fine big house. I heard there was water laid on, but you can't believe the half you hear. But water or no water, you've landed on your feet, Nancy. By the way, Davy John said Frank was coming round at seven to take you to the Pictures in Downpatrick. Ballynahinch isn't good enough for ye, now!'

Nancy sprang to her feet. 'Why didn't you say that before? Will you look at the time? It's well I have my Sunday clothes on me, but I must wash my face. Bessie, there's a hole in my stocking. Maybe you'd darn it for me? I'll bring you home some sweeties if Frank gives me any.'

Bessie went dutifully to fetch the chocolate box which held the family repair outfit, and Nancy having peeled off the damaged stocking, proceeded with her washing operations. 'Here's Peter,' she called from the sink. 'Let him get his own tea. He does little enough, the Lord knows.'

Mrs Montgomery rose and set about preparing her son's tea. Even her pride in her eldest daughter was a small thing in comparison with her affection for her only son. 'Is that you, Peter, boy? You must be starved. Come away and take your tea. I'm going to boil an egg for you.'

Peter Montgomery was certainly different from the rest of the family. He was a tall, slight youth of nineteen with fair curly hair and good features. He was well dressed, exceptionally so, when one considered his mother's circumstances and the fact that he had no job. There was a complete absence of Nancy's mistakes in the sartorial line. It was difficult to credit that this bored looking young man was anything but a chance visitor. 'Thanks, but I am not hungry. A cup of tea will do quite well.'

Nancy appeared at the door of the scullery and sniffed at him. She had no very high opinion of her brother. He could not get a job and he put on airs – both deadly sins in Nancy's eyes. Also the way he spoke and his general appearance annoyed her. 'Let him go and get it himself ... Coming strolling in here like Lord Muck, as if nobody had anything to do but dance attendance on him.'

Peter smiled, a very charming but not particularly frank smile. 'I heard Nancy was engaged. It seems to have ruffled her temper more than usual. But since you are so interested in my affairs, my dear Anna, you may be pleased to hear that I am no longer unemployed.'

Mrs Montgomery gasped. 'You've got a job, Peter? Where?'

Nancy laughed jeeringly. 'Shooting pheasants on somebody's estate – until the gamekeeper gets him. That's about all the job you'll ever get. Anything else is too much like work for your taste.'

'Nancy, be quiet,' said Mrs Montgomery sharply. 'Peter, I hope you have no taken a labouring job; you have no the strength for it.'

'No, indeed,' said Nancy, 'nor the stomach either. When you see Peter labouring, you'll see the hens giving milk.'

'Nancy is correct, as usual,' said Peter. 'The position I have obtained is not a labouring one. Mr Harkness has just appointed me junior clerk in the mill. I chanced to get a hint this afternoon that somebody was to be appointed. I called in and was lucky enough to meet Mr John Harkness, who was just leaving. I believe he had already had an interview with Nancy here. I am afraid that she had not given him a favourable impression of the family, and apart from that, he was somewhat prejudiced against appointing a local person to the clerical end of the business. He considers that such a procedure is bad for the discipline of the place. However, I persuaded him that I was suited for the post, and he agreed to overlook his rule in this particular case.'

'Very nice of him,' said Nancy viciously. 'You'll get about ten bob a week.'

Peter shook his head. 'Oh, no. As I have some theoretical knowledge of book keeping, and am older than the ordinary beginner, Mr Harkness offered me a commencing salary of two pounds a week. It is a beginning, and, of course, it will be increased as my value to the firm is realised.'

Mrs Montgomery staggered to a chair. The events of the day had been too much for her. For the moment the speed with which her rewards were arriving had bereft her of the power of speech.

Even Nancy's wit failed her. She picked up her coat. 'Give me that stocking, Bessie,' she said. 'I'll go along the road to meet Frank.'

CHAPTER TWO

On the evening following his interview with Nancy Montgomery, John Harkness dined with his two sons and Edward's wife, Margaret.

Margaret Harkness had been a Norton before her marriage, and though John Harkness had always regarded her father as one of his worst enemies (the Nortons were also in the spinning business), he thoroughly approved of the marriage, of Margaret herself, and more especially of their three sturdy sons. It was his constant regret that Charles showed no inclination to settle down to domestic bliss in anything like as suitable a manner. As he watched the lovely face of the gracious woman who was the mother of his grandchildren, and listened to her shrewd comments on the advantages of artificial silk over linen, he stifled a sigh. Charles would never have the sense to make so happy a choice. There was a thrawn streak in Charles, and he had no stability. He met everything trivial or significant with the same flippant levity. For all his apparent boyishness it was impossible to know what he really thought or felt – if he thought or felt at all. Yet he was his father's favourite, though the old man hid his preference well under a constantly reproving tongue. He was a little ashamed of his weakness where Charles was concerned. John Harkness was a man who resented weakness. He openly permitted himself to be sentimental towards his last born, his daughter, Marie, who, nearly twenty years before had cost his wife her life. Marie was a girl, and being so much younger than his sons, it accorded with his code to treat her with affectionate indulgence. But he was intolerant of the very idea of any of the men of the Harkness family needing such indulgence.

When Margaret had left the table, he glanced at his sons. 'I have made an appointment this afternoon about which I would like your opinion. We needed a new clerk, one who might later be able to fill Davidson's place when he is promoted on the retirement of Mr Seed. You may recall that Seed mentioned the case of a girl who was dismissed for a breach of discipline. I saw the girl – the circumstances were somewhat exceptional. I learned that she was the only member of her family in employment. I realise that she was an uneducated girl and spoke to me under the stress of considerable excitement; but, at the same time, I could not overlook the fact that she spoke in a most unseemly manner. I may be old-fashioned, Charles, but there is a relationship between employer and employee which must be maintained – no matter what the circumstances. I could, therefore, do nothing as far as the girl herself was concerned. You were about to make a remark, Charles? No? Well, perhaps, I may continue. Before I left the mill, this girl's brother called to see me. Before I go further, I may say, that I was considerably surprised to hear that the young man I interviewed was any relation to Nancy Montgomery. He appeared, in every way, a most suitable young man for the position he sought – that of junior clerk. I had some doubts as to the wisdom of appointing a local man, especially a brother of one of our former mill hands; but it appeared to me that this young man had risen considerably above his circumstances. I was also influenced by the fact that I had been compelled to exercise severity in the girl's case. I, therefore, made the appointment without consulting my co-directors.' He smiled, this being his idea of a neat joke.

Edward looked doubtful. 'I am not doubting your judgement, father. But the position is more than that of a junior clerk, it is that of secretary to the Ringawoody Spinning Mill, or will be shortly. Do you think that a brother of a girl from one of the spinning rooms is quite the person for such a position?'

Charles laughed. 'Edward is right, dad. This is a question of maintaining discipline. The prestige of the mill is at stake.'

John Harkness ignored Charles and turned to his elder son. 'I can assure you that that aspect received my attention. I think, however, that when you see the young man in question you will agree that he is entirely suitable. I think we can leave it at that.'

'Very well,' agreed Edward. 'I hope you are being wise. This is more the type of gesture we might expect from Charles here.'

'No damn fear it isn't,' said Charles. 'If I had anything so inconvenient as a conscience, I should not dream of trying to salve it by smiling on Peter because I had frowned on Paul. That strikes me as being dashed unfair to Paul and unnecessarily generous to Peter.'

John Harkness shook his head. 'I hope that I am not devoid of conscience, but the dismissal of the girl Montgomery does not trouble me in the slightest. However, I trust that I am just, and, when possible, I like to give every consideration to the people who are dependent on the mill for a livelihood.'

Charles raised his glass. 'Hear! hear! Your sentiments do you honour, sir. I drink to the Head of the Firm. Long may he rule us.'

Edward grinned and drank. Then he glanced at his father with a faintly malicious smile. 'To the Harkness discipline,' he said.

'Tempered with justice,' amended Charles, with mock gravity. 'Come on, dad. Drink to your downfall. You've brought it on yourself, so you may as well be sporting about it.' He smiled at his brother. 'The old pater is finished. He's getting just. A bad sign!'

John Harkness drank. 'And now,' he said, 'if you children have finished amusing yourselves we might join Margaret. We have forgotten that she is alone.'

'By the way where is Marie?' asked Edward rising.

'Marie,' explained Charles, 'is speaking for the Motion "That uncivilized man was happier than his so-called civilized descendant" at Ballyafton Presyterian Church Debating Society. You see that somebody in the family does take life seriously.'

'Has she given up the League of Nations?'

'Oh, yes,' said Charles, 'ages ago. She's had quite decent attacks of "United Ireland", "Equality for Women" and "Anti-Stag hunting" since that.'

'She has not yet taken up the art of cheeking her father, which is something to be grateful for,' said John Harkness as they left the diningroom.

Marie Harkness arrived at 'Craigaveagh' a few minutes after the return of her father and brother, and immediately rushed into the lounge where the two men were smoking. Marie, who was not yet twenty, was like most girls of her age, a bewildering mixture of the sophisticated young woman of her time and the ordinary crude, somewhat self-opinionated youngster, whose half-baked aggressiveness is so readily pardoned.

Marie was not good-looking. She had black hair which, alas, bore no resemblance to a raven's wing, and worn as Marie was wearing it, at the moment, made her look a bit like one of those little, sawdust filled dolls with china heads, which we used to buy for a halfpenny when we were children. She had a nice forehead which was completely covered by the heavy, dolly fringe and attractive grey eyes, but otherwise she was pale and somewhat nondescript. She put out her tongue at Charles, with whom she was always on excellent terms and installed herself on her father's knees.

'Daddy, we had a perfectly foul meeting. Remember all the trouble I took with my paper?'

'We remember all the trouble you gave everyone else at any rate,' said Charles.

'Speak when you're spoken to,' said Marie. 'I was addressing your father. Didn't I work hard at it, daddy?'

'Of course you did. Didn't it go down well?'

'Oh, it went all right. Everybody clapped like anything, and the minister said it showed "original thought and considerable ability". Wasn't that nice?'

'Very nice,' said her father. 'But what is the trouble then?'

'Well, after the speeches people got up to take sides. You know the way they do at a debate? Nearly everyone took my side at first, but then a young man from Ringawoody got up. Imagine a man from Ringawoody speaking at a debate! And do you know, he went on for nearly half-an-hour and he proved that everything I said was nonsense.'

'I could have done that in less than half-an-hour,' murmured the irrepressible Charles.

John Harkness laughed. 'Never mind, my dear. He was just showing off. I expect he talked nonsense, too.'

Marie shook her head. 'No, he did not. I wish I had known somebody like that was going to speak, and I would have been more careful. He won over all the votes for the other side. We only got seven. Terrible, wasn't it?'

'Who was he?' asked Charles.

'I can't quite place him,' said his sister. 'Somebody told me that his name was Montgomery – Peter Montgontery. I think he is one of the Montgomerys from Morton Lodge. Do you know him, daddy? And what on earth is he doing in Ringawoody?'

Charles roared. 'Don't let Morton Lodge hear you at that. Peter used to live in the second last house in the Mill Row. That was before his sister lost her job for using bad language in the spinning room. I don't know where they hang out now.'

Marie stared at him in unbelief. 'I don't believe you ... It's impossible.'

'No,' intervened her father. 'It is perfectly correct. I have just taken the young man into the office. But while there is no doubt that he comes from ordinary working-class people he is certainly a most remarkable young fellow. I was most favourably impressed by him.'

Marie veered round. 'Of course, I have always maintained that you find the highest standard of intelligence and the most genuine form of culture among the working people.'

'Marie is now about to have a brand new disease – the rights of the common people,' said Charles yawning. 'But I heartily second the motion. Look at Paddy Donovan! Not to mention that worthy beer-drinker, Jimmy McCarthy. Dad, did you know that Jimmy holds the championship for beer drinking in the County Down? They sent a man up from Lecale to tackle him. Jimmy cost his backers nine and eightpence after the Lecale man had been sick three times. There's good stuff in Jimmy, gallons of it.'

'You are vulgar and disgusting without being funny,' Marie informed him coldly. 'But all the same I think Peter Montgomery is splendid, and I am sure he will be most useful in the Debating Society.'

The year following old Mr Seed's retirement from the firm of Harkness, Harkness and Harkness was a most depressing one for the linen business.

Harkness's did their best, but they were losing heavily. Davidson, the new manager, though he worked hard, had peculiar ways, which did nothing to increase the rapidly diminishing orders. Young Montgomery, promoted to secretary before his twenty-first birthday, was more successful. Actually he did more than half the manager's work, but even he could not cope with the effects of the depression which increasingly darkened the once proud and healthy face of the textile industry.

Scutch mills failed, bringing down with them many a decent, hard-working man who, ignoring the warning of vanished profits, continued to pin his faith to the revival of flax growing, and pour out the savings of the good years. But faith availed him nothing. Savings were sooner or later all swallowed up. Scutching was finished, for the present at any rate.

Farming, too, was at its worst. Most of the farmers round Ballynahinch had depended a good deal on the flax crop. Many of them had owned or had shares in scutch mills, from which they reckoned to obtain the wherewithal to meet the heavy taxes which most of them had to bear under the land purchase scheme. With this source of income withdrawn, and, withdrawn under circumstances incurring disastrous losses, for scutching was dying a slow and expensive death, and with the ordinary income from the land down, as it was, to a devastatingly low level, things were pretty bad.

In the November following Peter Montgomery's promotion to the position of secretary at Ringawoody, the Hiring Fair in Ballynahinch presented a pathetic sight. The auctioneer's hammer had fallen repeatedly in the months previous. 'Farm for sale.' 'Farm for sale.' 'Farm for sale.' Brief notice of a long and tragic tale of gallant struggle, unceasing loss and ultimate ruin. But the spirit of the Northerner is not easily broken. The bank might sell up the family holding. Times would improve and land could always be bought back. In the meantime all who were able to work flocked to the Hiring Fair, and, if the young men and girls who crowded the Market Square in search of unaccustomed masters looked graver than usual, they held themselves erect and faced the new conditions with courage.

Frank Orr was at the Fair looking for a girl for Nancy, who was expecting a baby and was not quite up to her usual working form. In spite of the general depression Frank and Nancy had prospered. Frank was a good farmer with more sense of anticipation than the average conservative country man. He had got out of flax in time to avoid appreciable loss, and his marriage with Nancy had been one of the luckiest actions of a not particularly ill-omened life. Nancy was a born manager. Farm life suited her. She throve on hard work. She spared herself no effort for the improvement of Ballycam. She enjoyed being her own boss – and Frank's too, of course. She was radiantly happy, and infused the whole farm with an atmosphere of exultant, healthy wellbeing. She had scorned the idea that she required a girl to help her with the indoor work. She would be no spoilt wife to snatch at a commonplace happening as an excuse for pleading indisposition and indulging in laziness. But Frank, who esteemed her opinion in most things, rejected it on this particular point, and Nancy had given a very ungracious consent when she saw there was no moving of him.

Frank looked over the crowd. There would be little difficulty about getting a girl today. He could get a score at almost any terms he cared to offer. He moved forward suddenly. 'Why, if it isn't little Isobel Martin? How are you doing, Isobel? We were downright sorry to hear about your poor father. Everybody was. I never saw the like of his funeral.'

A pretty girl of some twenty-four years turned quickly. 'Frank Orr! I did not expect to see you here. How is Nancy? I heard that she was not very well.'

Frank shook his head. 'Nancy is grand. Her complaint is not very serious. But what are you doing here? I thought you were with your uncle in Dromara?'

'I'm looking for a job, Frank. My uncle in Dromara has more than enough to keep the farm going. Know anyone looking for a strong, respectable girl, who can cook, wash, milk, and mind the baby if necessary? Have you a girl at Ballycam?'

'No, and I'm seeking one,' said Frank slowly.

'Splendid,' said Isobel. 'I'll come for twenty-four pounds a year. I was going to ask thirty, but since you are an old friend ...'

Frank Orr looked troubled. 'I'm sorry, Isobel, I couldn't ...'

'Nonsense. Why not? I must get a job. I'd rather work for you and Nancy than someone I don't know. I could take advantage more, when I felt lazy.'

'I will not hire Hugh Martin's daughter as a servant in my house. But surely Isobel, with your education ...'

'Frank, with my education ... not to mention my Domestic Economy Course ... I'm not worth twopence on the labour market. There are thousands like me. Most of them have certificates too, whereas I have none. I might get a few shillings a week in an office, but that wouldn't pay my lodgings. Why should I not do what I can do best? Besides, I really like housework, and I can do it well. Give me a try.'

'I would not think of it. Did your father leave nothing?'

'About five hundred pounds of debt. It wasn't his fault. He put every penny he had into that old scutch mill. Talk about leaking buckets!'

'What did the farm go for?'

'Under a thousand. And he paid three thousand for that farm. The bank had fifteen hundred on it. It was bad for them, too, but I can do nothing about that in the meantime.'

Frank looked distressed. 'It's worse than I thought. Where are the two wee ladies?'

'Bridgit has gone to my Aunt Mary in Liverpool. She is going to keep her at school, and Tessie has gone to Cork to a cousin of my mother's. She is clever, and we think she might pass the Civil Service examination next year. But I must earn my own living; I could not possibly foist myself off on the Dromara folk indefinitely. By the look of things they won't be there very long.'

'My God! Is it as bad as that? No word of you marrying?'

Isobel laughed gaily. 'Unfortunately, not a word. Nancy Montgomery grabbed my man.'

Frank grinned. 'You showed little inclination to do any grabbing when you had the chance. Many's the better man than me you turned down. You were too ill to please.'

'And now I'm left high and dry,' said Isobel cheerfully. 'Well, if you won't give me a job I must be moving. Give my love to Nancy, and don't forget to invite me to the christening.'

Frank shook hands. 'You would not care to come and stay with Nancy for a bit – as a guest?'

Isobel shook her head. 'Thanks. No. I have no time for visiting.'

When Frank returned that evening with a buxom country lassie, he told Nancy of his encounter with Hugh Martin's daughter.

Nancy considered the matter in her practical way. 'You might have taken her for a bit. She could have taught me a lot. Isobel Martin was a great cook. It would have been nicer than having a stranger in the house.' She glanced disparagingly towards the stairs, which Eliza, the new arrival, had just ascended.

'But, Hugh Martin's daughter, Nancy I wouldn't feel comfortable about it.'

'And you feel comfortable when she's maybe going to people who don't know how she was reared? Men have the queer notions and no mistake. "What the eye does not see no upsets the stomach!" I'd have treated her right, and I'd have been real honoured to have her. Do you know if she was hired?'

Frank shook his head. 'I wouldn't say it. None of the farmers in Ballynahinch today would hire her, if I know anything about them. I'm fair upset about it.'

'That'll give the girl a poor breakfast. I'll tell you what, Frank, you might run me into Downpatrick?'

Frank looked bewildered. 'This evening?'

'Aye, why not? We've got a maid now. I've taken a notion to go to the Pictures and I want to see Peter. Did I tell you that he's staying in a grand hotel these days. His mother's house was no good enough for him. Not but that she's well rid of yon rubbish. Mr Montgomery has got a car now to go to the office. My, but we're quare and well set up! Yon lad would build a nest in your ear if you gave him the chance. I wish old man Harkness joy of his secretary.'

Frank rose lazily. 'I wish you had taken the notion before I put away our old "tin Lizzie". And why the notion to see Peter? You don't seem too fond of each other.'

'Aye, and you've said it,' said Nancy. 'But I may as well make what little use of him I can. I'm going to get Isobel Martin a job, if you must know.'

Frank paused at the door, opened his mouth to speak and changed his mind. Times had changed. He could do nothing for Hugh Martin's daughter. He would leave it to Nancy. The women seemed to think they could arrange their own affairs these days, and maybe they could, and, putting the whole business from him with a sigh of relief, he went out to give instructions to the boy.

Half-an-hour later, Nancy left Frank at the Post Office and made her way to Peter's hotel. She found him alone in the lounge, engaged in writing letters.

'And how is yourself?' she asked, assuming her broadest Downshire to annoy him. Though as far as that went her normal accent annoyed her brother almost as much as she could have desired.

Peter glanced up. 'This is an unexpected pleasure. Won't you sit down?'

'I don't mind if I do,' said Nancy, glancing round her with purely fictitious admiration. 'My, but you have the grand place here, Peter! Change for you after the old kitchen, isn't it? Though I always think there's something right cosy about a kitchen range. Not what you'd call stylish, maybe, but snug. Is that one of they electric fires?'

'Yes, that is an electric fire,' said Peter briefly. 'And, I may say that if you have merely called to admire the furniture, the place, as far as I know, is not for sale, and I happen to be busy.'

Nancy smiled affably and settled herself comfortably in her chair. 'Wonderful are the works of a wheelbarrow! But you always liked to ape the big fellow, didn't you, Peter? Sure, I'm the only woman in Ireland as sees you for what you are – a little wood and a lot of grease. Slippery, was the way I aye thought you. Still you keep moving, see now as you don't slip.'

Peter knew that she was deliberately baiting him in an effort to make him lose his temper. 'Come, Nancy, you have not come here in order to tell me what you think of me. You are not in the habit of wasting your own time, whatever you may do with other people's; besides, if I do not know already, it certainly is not from want of telling. What do you want?'

'You didn't think I maybe just wanted to have a look at you?'

'I did not.'

'And you're right. I could manage bravely without the pleasure. I want you to get a job for Isobel Martin.'

'Why did you not approach Mr Davidson? He is the manager.'

'Is he now? Well, knowing your little weakness for being the man who blows the whistle, I thought as I'd see you first. Mr Davidson would take her on if you asked him. Aren't you the white haired boy? And, between ourselves – I'm thinking yon Davidson is going astray in the head.'

Peter looked at her curiously. 'What makes you say that?'

'I've eyes in my head and ears, too. He went into Biddy Griffith's last week and asked for forty-seven boxes of sherbert. Forty-seven boxes! Biddy had none in stock, being as it was winter; and he said as he would report her to the Cabinet. If that's not "bats in the belfry" it's something mighty quare.'

Peter laughed. 'He was only joking.'

'Joking!' said Nancy. 'Did you or anyone in Ringawoody ever hear tell of a joke from Davidson? I suppose it was another joke when he walks up to poor Jean McCrea in the packing room and told her as the Lord God would strike her blind in the night? John Harkness has the right selection in his mill, so he has!'

Peter brushed the matter away easily. 'Davidson is just odd. Now what is this about Isobel Martin?'

'She's looking for a job. You knew Hugh Martin died sudden – like two months ago.'

Peter nodded. 'Yes, I was at the funeral. But Hugh Martin was worth any amount of money. Why should Isobel be looking for a job?'

'He *was*, but not yesterday or the day before. That scutch mill ruined him and kiled him forby. There's no a red cent left for the girls. The bank took all and was no out of it very well at that.'

Peter lit a cigarette. 'I daresay that I could get her a job, but Isobel Martin will not like working in the mill, and we do not employ girls in the office.'

'Isobel Martin is a well-reared girl, not a poor blown-up creature as has to be aye minding what she does in case the folks would no see that she was a lady. Isobel Martin has no to think that highly of herself, others will do it without being reminded, and it would no matter the skin of a tattie if she was working in the mill or was M.P. for East Down.'

Peter shrugged. 'That's as may be. But Mr Harkness had business dealings with Hugh Martin and thought very highly of him, I am sure he would not like it.'

'Then don't tell him. He doesn't ask for the family history of every girl in the place. The girl must get a job, and she'd get better paid in the mill than in service.'

Peter knew that he would not get rid of Nancy unless he agreed. Though he disliked her intensely, she was the only person he knew to whom he accorded a measure of genuine respect, which, in this case, was closely akin to fear. He had never been able to deceive Nancy. It was probably true that she was the only woman of his acquaintance who refused to take him at his face value. A counterfeit, no matter how accurately forged, fears the over-discerning eye. He knew that Nancy saw through him; but even he himself did not quite realise the disgusted contempt with which she regarded what she saw. Nancy did not bother weighing up his character or counting his vices and virtues. She just knew that he was no good. 'Very well, I think I can promise you that she will be given a job. By the way, Nancy, I thought of trying to get a house somewhere else for mother and the girls.'

Nancy flashed round on him. 'Oh, did you? I suppose they are too near to suit your convenience. Reflect on your grand social standing, maybe!'

'That is not the point,' said Peter quietly. 'That cottage is uncomfortable and insanitary. I hoped that since circumstances have been improved for both you and me we might do something for the others.'

'So that's the idea! You get the house and I pay the rent. Like one of your bargains, that is!'

Peter restrained his temper. 'I am prepared to contribute my share.'

'Your share!' Nancy laughed shrilly. 'So it's now you're thinking of your mother – the woman who nearly starved herself for you. She tries to shield you, but I know rightly you haven't given her one penny in all this time. Frank already gives her as much as he can afford. I'm no asking him to give more so as you can get the mother who would let you wipe your boots on her, out of your sight.'

'That is not so, Nancy. It is true that I have not been in a position to help up to now because I have had heavy expenses. If you feel that you are already doing as much as you can, I shall try to provide a more suitable house on my own.'

'Where were you thinking of?' asked Nancy.

'I thought, perhaps, Belfast.'

Nancy rose. 'Trust you to think of something good. Don't you wish you could rise to Timbuctoo – and send me with them? Good evening to you, Peter. Don't forget about Isobel Martin, or I'll be back; and that would no suit either of us.'

As Nancy and Frank came out from the Pictures some hours later, a big, grey car swept past the Post Office, turned up English Street, and stopped at Frank's hotel.

'That's one of the Harkness's cars,' said Frank. 'Is that Peter who got out?'

'It is,' said Nancy. 'He's been in high society the night.'

Frank was slow at getting the car started, but for once Nancy was not impatient. She watched the big, grey car back up the street and turn. As it flashed past she eyed it closely. The car was empty – save for the girl at the wheel. And the girl at the wheel was Marie Harkness.

'That explains the emigration of the family!' said Nancy to herself with a little smile. 'Devil mend old John Harkness. He's been asking for this for a long, long time.'

CHAPTER THREE

Marie Harkness had called for Peter earlier in the evening. As, secretary of the Debating Society, she had arranged that Peter should speak on this particular evening. Marie did not like having her plans upset. When Peter had 'phoned her from the mill, in the course of the day, and pleaded to be excused, as his car was in the process of being decarbonised, she had promptly informed him that that was no excuse. She would see that he was taken to Ballyafton and back again. As she had no time to make other arrangements she had decided to drive herself. The debate went splendidly, and Peter was the hero of the evening. On the way home, Marie, who regarded his success as a personal triumph, was in the highest spirits. Peter, realising that he was letting an unique opportunity pass, cursed the circumstances which forced him to an excessive caution.

Peter Montgomery was not in love with his employer's daughter, though he had thought of her a great deal since he had first noticed her at the Debating Society. In the months that followed, he had frequently cast round in his mind for a circumspect method of establishing himself on a more friendly footing. He liked to remind himself that he had been attracted to Marie before he actually knew who she was. If this were not quite true, it was as true as many of the beliefs Peter Montgomery managed to entertain about his own motives. Like most natural liars, Peter was untruthful with himself. True, Marie was a cheery little specimen and a likeable individual. Peter probably liked her in so far as he was capable of liking anyone other than Peter Montgomery, but Peter could have liked a polecat if he imagined that his personal progress would be thereby accelerated.

Marie, on the other hand, was incurably romantic, and she was not without a streak of snobbery. She rather liked the role of the employer's daughter being nice to the superior type of employee. While she was not in love with Peter, she was very much in love with the idea of being in love with him. She would hardly have been feminine had she been completely insensible to Peter's attractions – his courteous attentions, his respectful admiration, his obvious efforts to please her. As Marie saw it, Peter was shy because he was poor. In her opinion that was entirely suitable and very romantic. The really fine type of man always felt like that. Marie was perfectly convinced that Peter was a really fine type of man. With such an attractive face he could hardly be anything else.

As they approached the Spa Roadhouse, Marie slowed down. 'Let's go and have some coffee,' she suggested.

Peter shook his head. 'No, not here. Your father wouldn't like it, Miss Harkness.'

Marie pouted and drove on. 'He wouldn't mind. I've often had coffee at the Roadhouse.'

Peter smiled. 'Yes but not with me. It's not the Roadhouse but the company to which he might object.'

Marie glanced at him provocatively. 'Aren't you very humble, all of a sudden?'

'Not in the slightest. But I should be sorry to be the cause of any unpleasantness between yourself and your father. I think too highly of you to expose you to even a domestic row.' He smiled and Marie blushed. This was not quite what she had expected, but it was going to be very interesting.

'My father thinks very highly of you,' said Marie seriously. 'He is not a bit like what you think.'

'What do I think?' demanded Peter.

Marie had an idea that this scene in the pretty little play she had imagined was getting beyond her control. She was annoyed with herself for getting flustered so easily, and she was a little cross with Peter for not knowing his lines better. 'Oh, I don't know exactly. But you speak as though he were the fearfully heavy father sort of person. He's not a bit. Daddy would let me do anything I liked.'

Peter laughed softly. 'Don't you believe it, young lady! Have you ever tried to do anything of which your father did not approve?'

'Often, but I always persuade him in the end that he does approve.'

'And if you wanted to do something very badly, of which you knew he would never really approve?' asked Peter.

'But I don't,' said Marie uncertainly.

'But I do,' said Peter. 'I want to know you better. I'd like to see you sometimes, talk to you – take you places. There doesn't seem to be much harm in that, but your father would not approve.'

Marie turned to him with childish sincerity. 'There wouldn't be any harm in it, and I am sure if daddy knew you – even as well as I do – that he would not mind. But I should not like to do anything without telling him.'

Peter sighed. 'That is out of the question in the meantime.'

They were approaching Downpatrick, and realising that his chance was almost gone Peter made a last effort. 'Let me take you to a show in the city on Saturday. Then if you decide that seeing me without your father's permission is wrong, I shall not ask you again. Please say yes.'

Marie gazed at him with troubled eyes. 'I don't like it, Peter, but I'll come on Saturday.'

'That's fine,' said Peter. 'I'll meet you at the Junction at 7 o'clock.'

Nancy called with her mother the week before Christmas. She was laden with parcels, including a turkey for the Christmas dinner and gifts for the three girls.

Eileen and May, the two youngest, were decorating the kitchen with masses of evergreens, and Bessie was giving instructions. Mrs Montgomery was baking in preparation for the Christmas festivities.

All hands downed tools when Nancy appeared, and there was a hearty, if noisy, greeting for her.

'Ooh! It's Nancy, and she's got ever so many parcels,' cried Eileen enthusiastically. 'Nancy, look at all the berries on the holly. Me and May walked all the way to Seaforde for it, and the gardener gave us a great big bunch of chrysanthemums, and we're having a party on Christmas Eve, and you're coming and Frank and everyone ...'

'God bless the child! What a tongue! How are you, mother? You're looking fine.'

'I'm grand, and the girls were never better. Come up to the fire and taste my mince pies. I'll make a wee sup of tea.'

'Heard anything from your grand son?' asked Nancy.

Mrs Montgomery set down the teapot carefully. 'Now, isn't it strange you asked! Nancy, I know you've been the good daughter to me since you was that high, but you wrong Peter. Peter's had a sore lot of expense. Sure he must keep up his position. I could live on the envy of the folk, if 'twas nothing else. Fair jumping out of their skins they are. The face on yon Moore woman near puts the milk sour these days. But I was telling you about the news I had in from Peter … He's for getting me a grand house in Belfast with a proper scullery and a gas cooker. I knew Peter would not forget his mother. Oh, but I'm the proud woman these days, Nancy. I hope the Lord will no count it to me, but sure it would be agin human nature no to be proud of children like mine.'

'I'll be sorry to see you go so far,' said Nancy. 'When are you for flitting?'

'The end week in January. Peter'll fix it all.'

'Has he been over?' Nancy asked carelessly.

Mrs Montgomery's face lost something of its brightness. 'No, but he's terrible busy. You and Frank will come over on Christmas Eve, Nancy? I'm for having a wee bit of a party, and I would like fine for the neighbours to see you and Frank and how bravely we are all doing.'

'Of course, ma, we'll love to. Did you ask Peter?'

'Peter is going to a party … somewhere else. He promised before I mentioned it. It's but natural, he's greatly sought on … though I would have liked fine for the neighbours to see him in the house. They have bad, bitter tongues to them, Nancy. Envy it is, envy and spite. By the way, I hear talk of an Orange demonstration. I wouldn't doubt there'll be more trouble.'

Nancy shrugged. 'We're great ones for the religion and the fighting. If it spreads to Ringawoody Mr Harkness will be for closing down. They say he threatened it before in the "trouble". That kept them quiet, I can tell you.'

'It did,' said Mrs Montgomery reflectively. 'I mind it well. Things were that slow in Ringawoody ye would hardly know there was a war on at all. But old Father O'Brien was alive in them days. Eh! But he was the right man, and aye for peace. I mind when Meg Round-over-the-hill (God help her! She was never right in the head), put on the orange blouse … if you'd seen the sight of her, and herself with a skirt like the Spa Golf Course. Old Jamie McCreevy stops dead in front of her and shouts out: "Up the Republic!" The girls were coming down the loanin' from the mill, a wild set they were in them days, and ready as a loaded gun to take sides. His reverence comes across the road, seventy he was, aye and past it. "See here, Jamie McCreevy," he says, "if ye don't shut that rat-trap of yours, it's my stick will be up and when it comes down it will be on the back of Jamie McCreevy. I'll not leave a whole bone in your lint-hole of a carcass," he says. Lord, but he was the grand man, Papish or no. Even the Orangemen were feared of him. They nearly fought rings round them to get drumming at his burying. And sure I don't believe Father O'Brien would have minded. 'Tisn't every Papish priest would get the Orange lads to make an offer like yon.'

'I liked him fine,' said Nancy. 'We used to steal his apples. He caught me one day, and he says, "Now, don't be tearing your clothes on that wall, lassie. Just come in by the front gate." I never had a notion for an apple since. It's a pity if they are for starting more trouble now. Me and Frank make it out smooth enough with our neighbours. We've no time for fighting, all this history is ruining the people. I would no say it outside, ma, but that drumming would split the head of Slieve Donard. The Protestants would be the first to complain, but they wouldn't please the others to give way to them.'

Mrs Montgomery shook her head. 'There's something of it, but it no does to say all you think. But it's comforting to know the drums are fit to drown the harps still.'

Nancy had arranged to meet Eileen and May in Ballynahinch in order to take them to the Pictures. When she left the bus and saw the crowded streets she wished herself and the children safely home. There were a large number of drunks already among the crowd, and she could see no sign of the little girls.

A farmer from the Hollows came up to her as she was about to begin her search. 'Is that you, Mistress Orr? If I was you, woman, I'd away home on the next bus. There's going to be trouble in Ballynahinch before the night is through.'

'God bless us all!' said Nancy. 'Is that the way of it? I'm for home when I find the wee ladies. They were to meet me here, and devil a sign of them.'

'They'll be down town looking at the shops. Get them lifted and away back with ye all. Now, I'm telling ye.'

The farmer moved away and Nancy made her way heavily along the street. Unfamiliar faces were everywhere. The town was full of strangers, and very excited strangers by the sound of them. The crowd was pushing up the hill. Nancy was forced in the press in the opposite direction to which she wished to go. She was anxious about her sisters; if they were caught up in the crowd she might never find them.

At length the crowd came to a halt outside the Catholic church. Recalling her mother's story Nancy was thoroughly frightened. She felt sick and weary and she knew that she was in no condition for a rough and tumble. 'Let me out of this,' she gasped wildly.

A man glanced at her and pushed a way for her through the crowd. 'The way is clear there. The police will no interfere with you. Keep to the middle of the street and you'll be all right.'

Clear of the crush Nancy was able to see the position. The main body of the crowd was pressed against the far side of the street. A dozen or more policemen were standing round the church. A number were trying vainly to break up the crowd. At the moment the centre of the street was fairly clear. Nancy was about to retrace her steps, when to her horror she saw Eileen and May waving to her from the top of the church steps. The two children had evidently slipped past the police cordon and climbed the railings to see what all the fun was about. When the doors opened, if a fight began, they would be in the direct line of the missiles from both sides.

Frantically she pushed past the policeman who barred her way. Before he could prevent her she pushed open the heavy gates and rushed up the steps. The two children, realising that they were in for trouble from Nancy, darted past her. Dizzy with relief and excitement she saw a policeman grab a hand of each and lead them out of the confusion. She swayed unsteadily. Sergeant Green, who had seen the incident from the road was pushing his way towards her. He was too late.

Without warning, the church doors swung open. Nancy saw a menacing crowd above her and a no less menacing one below. For one moment there was a growling pause. Then a stone flung from the far side of the street struck the church wall. In a fraction of a second the fight was on. Stones were flying in all directions. The attacked party were evidently not altogether unprepared. The men were to the front, and they were well supplied with stones. For a brief minute the police were absolutely powerless.

Strengthened by her terror, Nancy glanced fearfully round her. She caught sight of a neighbouring farmer in the forefront of the church party. She rushed wildly towards bim, but a youth near him, mistaking her intention, thrust out at her roughly and sent her spinning down the steps, under the feet of the advancing throng in the street.

A woman's voice rang out from the door. 'Joe O'Kelly, that's Frank Orr's wife ... My God, and the way she is!'

O'Kelly, the farmer, uttered a deep oath and made down the steps, accompanied by the youth who had dealt the blow. Through a fusillade of tones from both directions they dragged the now unconscious Nancy from beneath the feet of the hysterical crowd.

The sergeant fought his way to the scene. 'I tried to reach her,' he gasped. 'She went in after those two brats of children. Is she hurt?'

O'Kelly shook his head. 'I couldn't say, sergeant. Try to clear a way and we'll get her out of this. I doubt you'll be needed here, for a bit. It's a wonderful country! Carry her easy now,' he ordered the youth, 'and if ill comes to Frank Orr's wife for this night's work, I'll go into the witness box myself to see you're hanged.'

The disturbance in Ballynahinch was soon quietened by the police. But Nancy Orr's son was born that night and died before morning.

'A Protestant the less!' said Nancy bitterly to Mrs O'Kelly, who had been with her all night. 'At least he'll be in no more rows.'

'You must no grieve, Nancy lass. It's the Lord's will,' said Mrs O'Kelly sadly.

'I'm no grieving,' said Nancy. 'I'll have other sons, but you should no be blaming the Lord in the wrong.'

Chapter Four

John Harkness summoned his workers together on the day following the Ballynahinch row. He strode to the platform at the end of the huge hall of the Workers' Recreation Club. White-haired, keen-eyed, he faced the mixed throng before him. Sullen murmurings gave way to silence. Old man Harkness had a way with him. 'I asked you to come here today,' he began, 'for two reasons. In the first place, as you are all aware, there has been some little trouble in a neighbouring town. We, like Ballynahinch, have our proportion of hooligans. I am speaking particularly to the wiser element. I strongly advise you to keep an eye on any such hooligans. I have already heard a few whispers which I do not want to hear repeated. I have no time for trouble and neither have you, if you attend to your work. I am not interested in the creeds of my employees. I am interested only in the quality of the yarn they spin. Ringawoody Mill is a spinning factory, not a bear garden. I warn you now, and I shall not repeat the warning – if I hear the least suggestion here of anything that might lead to a repetition of the disgraceful business that took place at Ballynahinch, I shall close the mill indefinitely. With regard to the other matter, there will be the usual two days' break for Christmas, and I take this opportunity of wishing you all a very Happy Christmas and a Bright and Prosperous New Year.'

Isobel Martin watched John Harkness depart. She sensed the pleasure his power gave him. It was so unnecessary to make such a speech. There had been no signs of trouble in Ringawoody. People might utter foolish remarks, but people were always doing that. She had not realised that she would resent John Harkness as a master. But she did. She was part of that crowd he could subdue, with a glance. She hated it.

The endless clatter of tongues – shrill, harsh, sibilant – tore at her frayed nerves. The crude, outspoken language of the mill still made her recoil. Isobel was used to the rough frankness of the farm. It was merely a question of habit. Strangers sickened at the stench from the lint hole; natives knew it to be necessary, and even went so far as to proclaim it healthy. In time she would tune her ears to the din of the mill and listen no longer for the old familiar sounds of the farm. The heavy odour of confined humanity would pass unnoticed; the monotony of the meaningless task cease to weary. She was independent, earning her living; a Martin could do no less or no more.

The crowd passed out. It was the mill dinner hour. Isobel had sandwiches, but little inclination to eat them. She stood at the street door, angry with herself for the queer nauseous weakness that assailed her, grateful for the brief moment of loneliness and the feel of the outside air. But her seclusion was not long undisturbed. A car pulled up at the door. She drew back a little as she saw Charles Harkness emerge. She had met him once or twice at dances and she shrank from recognition. A few days ago she would not have cared. The spirit of John Harkness's discipline had already touched her. Charles entered the hall without glancing in her direction, then seeing that the place was deserted he turned back. 'Do you know if Mr Harkness has left?' he asked her.

'I heard someone say that he had gone to Belfast,' said Isobel as naturally as she could manage … If he recognised her now, she would be sacked. Her nervousness in itself was enough to attract attention.

Charles looked at her with concern. 'I say, you are ill, aren't you? You look ghastly.'

Isobel was not long enough in the job to have learned the language. She smiled. 'That is not very complimentary. I am quite well I assure you.'

Charles looked at her closely. 'I beg your pardon. I thought you were one of the mill girls. Were you looking for someone?'

Isobel shook her head. 'No. I am one of the mill girls – even if I do look ghastly.'

Charles Harkness frowned. There was something decidedly odd about this. 'Mill girls are not expected to exchange pleasantries with the directors,' he informed her. 'And you ought not to be hanging about here. A newcomer I presume?' His words and tone had the desired effect of depriving Isobel of her discretion.

'Your presumption is accurate – if one can say no more of it. I was unaware that there was any rule against standing here. I shall try to remember. There are so many peculiar rules …'

Charles grinned. 'I knew your face was familiar. I danced with you at Ardglass Golf Club, in September, wasn't it? You're Miss Martin from the Knoll … the eldest one, Isobel. What on earth are you doing here?'

Isobel wondered desperately if there were any chance of persuading him to hold his tongue. It was not very likely, but it was worth trying. 'I cannot explain now. But please understand that it is most important for me that I should keep my job. It can make no possible difference to you, but if you mention it to your father he will not let me stay. At least wait until you have heard the facts.'

'Why not give me the facts now?'

Isobel was very near tears. 'There's no time, and I'm sick,' she said miserably. 'Please leave me alone. I'm not used to the place yet.'

'Here, you!' Charles called a boy from the packing yard. 'Go over to the office and tell Mr Davidson that I have sent ... the girl Martin home. Tell him she has been taken ill.'

'Very good, sir,' said the boy and departed on his errand.

'Could I find your coat?' Chares asked.

Isobel indicated the empty hall. 'It's on a chair at the back.'

When he had helped her on with her coat, he opened the door of the car. 'Where are you staying?'

'At Dromara with my uncle. But I am not going home with you. I shall need my bicycle for the morning.'

'You will not be coming here in the morning or any other morning unless you provide me with a little more information. You can please yourself.'

Isobel got in. 'I think you're terribly mean ... and everyone will talk so.'

'That's just too bad,' said Charles missing the gate by half an inch as he shot out into the road.

They drove on in silence for a few minutes and then Charles Harkness turned to his companion. 'I think I have the general outline. I knew Martin's scutch mill had failed, and I remember now hearing of your father's death.'

Isobel nodded. 'Would you like any further details?' she asked sarcastically.

He saw with relief that she was no longer in any danger of breaking down and he changed his tone. 'I'm fearfully sorry. It's most unpleasant for you. Please don't think I'm trying to make things more difficult or show my authority or any nonsense like that. But if it were my sister ...'

'If it were your sister she would just have to put up with it. I don't mind working, and anyway, I've got to do it. I've been looking for a job for a long time. I would have preferred housework. I have some training in that line, but none of the farmers round here would employ me because I am Hugh Martin's daughter. A very strange way of being kind, though I know they meant it well. I do not wish to leave the district while my uncle can hold on at Dromara. I hardly think it will be much longer. Then I shall look for a job somewhere else.'

'You really think you can stick it out there?'

Isobel raised her head proudly. 'I can stick anything. You need not worry on that score.'

Charles shook his head. 'I couldn't be a party to such an arrangement. I see your point, but you must try to see mine. I can't think of anything more unsuitable.'

Isobel recognised the old argument. She had not really expected anything else. 'Very well, Mr Harkness, I shall go. I don't suppose you can help being a snob ... as your father's son you could scarcely be otherwise. I do see your point. It is, of course, entirely unsuitable that anyone you ever chanced to meet – as – shall I say, a social equal should fall so low. In an indirect, involved way, that could only be comprehensible to a Harkness, it reflects slightly on yourself. But you need not have worried, as one of your father's workers, I should not have expected you to treat me as a social equal. In any case I am rather out of golfing circles these days.'

Charles swore inwardly. 'Trust a woman to hit below the belt. You can go or stay as you please. Your own attitude is about as snobbish as it could be, though I don't suppose you have the intelligence to realise it. But please understand this, Miss Martin. I make no promise to involve myself in any melodramatic, wild cat schemes to deceive my father. And, since you take it so much to heart, I am quite prepared to treat you as a social equal. You appear to have gone into the subject pretty deeply. I have not. I must look up a book on the subject. With "the upper ten" coming in as mill hands we directors have to brush up our social etiquette.'

Isobel ground her teeth in sheer temper but held her tongue. She had got her own way in the meantime and she would not risk reopening the argument.

They drove to Dromara in silence. Isobel got out at the farm. 'Will you kindly see that my bicycle is sent along on one of the lorries?' she said coldly.

'Certainly, madam. Anything else today, madam?'

Isobel did not deign to reply. She had begun to realise that Charles Harkness knew more than one way of dispensing with her services.

Charles Harkness, however, repented of his attitude. He had wished sincerely to be of assistance and he had been unnecessarily rude. He decided that something would have to be done regarding the girl's position but in the meantime he need not go out of his way to make the situation any worse.

When she returned to work Isobel received a note from him expressing regret for his discourtesy, and intimating that as far as he was concerned her position, while she wished to keep it, was perfectly safe. The note cheered her immensely. He was a decent sort after all, and obviously neither petty nor snobbish. She would have liked to have made a similar gesture and admitted provoking his discourtesy, but under the circumstances she thought better of this idea and contented herself with smiling at him, in what she hoped was an understanding, and, at the same time sufficiently distant manner. Charles appreciated her smiles, without translating them as fully as Isobel would have wished, and waited an opportunity to reopen the subject. That Isobel Martin's position was no business of his was an aspect of the case which he resolutely put aside; nor was he able to justify himself by the argument, that like his father, he identified himself with the mill so completely that every detail of its organisation was a matter of vital importance to him. Charles would have been amused had anyone described him as chivalrous, but no knight in armour, complete with horse and medieval background, was ever more enthusiastic about rescuing the lovely lady from the dragon. In a country still happily full enough of Charleses one could almost regret the perversity of the lady who refuses to regard the dragon with an adequate proportion of terror or the knight with the correct expression of gratitude.

Christmas passed pleasantly and uneventfully in Ringawoody. Christmas Clubs issued in bedroom slippers, silk scarves, bottles of perfume and children's toys, the shillings and sixpences that had so painstakingly been accumulated. Whiskey was drunk, puddings eaten, cakes cut and stomachs upset in the time-honoured manner. Mrs Montgomery had her party despite the absence of Peter and Nancy. The Moore woman insinuated that the absent son, and maybe the absent daughter, now thought themselves too grand for their poor mother. She was sympathetic on the subject of ingratitude, and the ill-rearing some young people proved to be. But Mrs Montgomery put this down to jealousy and pure spite, and refused to have her Christmas darkened by other folk's lack of charity.

There was the Protestant Christmas Tree and the Catholic Christmas Tree – the same tree redecorated, to save an extra journey to Seaforde. But this was not divulged by the secretary of either Christmas Tree Committee. One never knew what might or might not be taken as an insult. Church bells rang, and the village put on its new scarf and gloves and wended its way up the hill or across the Row, as the case might be.

There were a great many parties. Some people had select dances and others had ordinary ones. A number of people paid off heavy obligations by giving trifling gifts, but a larger number paid for trifling obligations by giving proportionately large gifts. Everybody gave and received a number of useless objects, but everybody enjoyed both operations very much, which, after all, is the main thing.

Ringawoody had one very useful Christmas custom. Many of the men went shooting on the marshes on Christmas Day. The old legend went that they were supposed to shoot the Christmas dinner. Sometimes they shot a few wild duck and an odd snipe, but the principal advantage of the custom nowadays was that theshoot took them out of the road of busy womenfolk while the great meal of the day was being prepared. Children played on the street and wished they had been given the toys of the children next door instead of their own. They also got colds in their heads, which, together with the Christmas fare, helped to bring down the attendance in the schools in the weeks that followed Christmas.

Behind the pleasant, homely, human scenes, the mill stood aloof and slightly sinister in its unaccustomed desertion, as though mocking in its silence the childish amusements of its creatures.

Finally, came the Mill Party, the big event of the village. John Harkness provided the Mill Party. All the Harkness family put in an appearance. All the big farmers who sold flax, or had sold flax, or even hoped to sell flax to Harkness, Harkness and Harkness, turned out. For once religion was no ban. Priest and Parsons led together on Michael and George alike. The children came with their fathers and mothers, uncles, aunts and cousins. People always prophesied that there would be trouble when it came to 'God Save the King' but were always disappointed.

First the children had a Christmas Tree. Children have little sense of loyalty, and they stated quite definitely that the Mill Christmas Tree was very much better than either the Catholic or Protestant one. When the gifts had been presented, they played, 'Here we come gathering nuts in May', 'Down on the carpet' and the 'Farmer wants a wife'.

Then Bridie Sullivan, Dan Murphy and Kathleen Moore sang 'O'Donnell Aboo' and Jane Hamilton, Margaret Bryson and Bessie Montgomery sang 'Derry Walls'. After which all the children joined forces in several songs dealing with wagons and horses and empty saddles.

Tea was the next item on the programme; a lengthy, messy, but thoroughly enjoyable affair. When the youngsters were too full to make any more noise or even to eat another morsel, Mr John Harkness made a speech – an excellent time for making a speech to children, if one holds the view that children listen to speeches. At this hour, they gave the appearance of attention because they lacked the energy to make shuffling sounds with their feet. Sometimes they sighed heavily, but that was due to repletion as much as boredom.

When the speech was over the children were taken home; the band arrived and the grownups danced. In the middle of the dancing there were rather a lot of other speeches and then more eating and more dancing. The procedure was pretty unvaried, and it was always a very good party.

Isobel Martin had not intended going to the Party. She pleaded that her father was not yet a year in his grave, and she did not feel inclined for parties, but the executive committee, which, in this case, was represented by Charles Harkness, put her in charge of the Christmas Tree and she had perforce to give way.

The mill was working again, but Peter Montgomery appeared in the spinning room, where Isobel was employed, and instructed the spinning master to release her in order that she might dress the Tree. Isobel, accordingly, betook herself to the Hall, which had been lavishly decorated the evening before. Finding that the toys had already arrived, she set to work in her usual efficient manner. She had scarcely begun when Charles Harkness arrived on the scene and offered his assistance. Isobel's heart sank, but she determined to do her best to avoid arguments concerning her job.

Charles laid himself out to put her fears at rest, and in a short time Isobel had completely forgotten that she was a mill hand and that Charles was one of the firm's directors. 'Who picked the toys?' she asked. 'They are just the kind of things children love.'

Charles was busy winding up a most convincing-looking racing car. 'By jove! Look how that goes, Isobel? What's that you said? Who picked the things? Margaret, she's my sister-in-law. You'd like her. She has three great youngsters. Marvellous kids they are. I'd like you to meet her and Marie.'

Isobel concentrated on the progress of the car with interest. 'I should like to,' she said absently. 'Is Marie your sister?'

'Yes. She goes in for things a lot, but she's a good sport. Why, what's wrong?'

Isobel's face had suddenly gone blank. She remembered, and, for the first time she remembered with bitterness and resentment, the alteration in her circumstances. She turned to the tree savagely. 'I'd almost forgotten.' In her exasperation with fate she had a childish inclination to hit out at someone ... anyone. 'I beg your pardon ... sir.'

Charles flushed. Had she known it, she could not have chosen a surer method of throwing him off his balance. 'Isobel, that's not fair. I know how you feel. That was the very thing I wished to guard against when I objected to you coming here.'

The girl sat down limply. 'I know. I'm sorry. Do you think anyone will come in, I'd like a cigarette? Thanks. Don't you smoke, if anyone comes you take mine.' She leaned against the platform and stared at the Tree. 'You have been fearfully decent. I honestly do appreciate it. I'm such a cat that when I'm fed up I just try to be annoying.

You mustn't imagine that I am unhappy or overworked or anything like that.'

Charles lit a cigarette gloomily, having already forgotten her order. 'I must say you look blissfully happy. And whether you are overworked or not you look tired and white. You always look ready to drop. It's not a question of work, it's a question of a certain kind of work. Isobel, please give it up.'

'I can't – not yet. But it won't be much longer. My uncle expects that the bank will take action in March ... I'll go then, I promise, no matter what happens. Though by then, I suppose I shall be used to it.'

'I won't have it! You must not get used to it,' said the man angrily.

She blushed. 'Isn't that my affair?'

He pulled her to her feet. 'Don't let's fight about it. Do you know you are right under that spray of mistletoe?'

She made as though to move, but he kissed her. She turned to the tree to hide her embarrassment. 'And I owe that to the mistletoe?' she said lightly.

Charles glanced up with a grin. 'I don't really think there is any mistletoe. In fact I am quite sure my father does not approve of mistletoe. It's bad for discipline, you know.'

The Mill Party was as successful as usual. Isobel enjoyed herself in an excited, nervous, half-fearful way. She was disturbed by the attentions of Charles, for she knew that they could scarcely pass without comment in a place like Ringawoody, where possible and impossible romances for Charles were always being invented. But with her native honesty she admitted to the more sensible Isobel Martin that the party would have been a dismal affair had he ignored her.

When the interlude for speech-making arrived, Isobel had her first big account rendered for the strain of the past months. The average intelligent individual can form a fair diagnosis of the health of his nerves by compelling himself to sit through a particularly long session of bad speeches made by verbose and uninteresting people about nothing that could be interesting to anyone.

The speeches at the Mill Party were bad, but they were not, by any means, the worst of their kind, and, since Isobel had attended many General Meetings, lunches and teas in connection with the Presbyterian Church she was not without a substantial training. Under normal circumstances she would have accepted the matter as a minor trial of patience.

The speech made by Mr John Harkness began the trouble. It exuded from every sentence John Harkness, his kingdom, his power and his glory. It wrapped itself round the mill with majestic dignity; it gradually unfolded to envelop the village with firm, but, as it was Christmas, not unkindly, patronage. It was the speech of a man, who realising that he has been selected by the Almighty for a high estate, accepts his heavy responsibility with courage.

There was much clapping, mostly because the speech was over. Isobel wondered desperately why murder was considered a serious crime.

But the worst was yet to come. The priest arose and spoke of John Harkness and his work and his mill; he spoke of the joy of labour, of duty, loyalty and gratitude; he returned to John Harkness, he spoke of his character, his high endeavour, his standards, the respect that was due to him as a fine gentleman and a just employer.

Isobel was now disgusted with her inability to control her rising irritation. She clenched her hands and tried to imagine the confusion that would ensue if she suddenly got up and gave vent to her rage. 'Idiot, imbecile, fool,' she muttered. 'I wish I knew more words ... He's going to stop ... no, he's off again ... My God, he's going back over it all again ... No, he isn't ...' She clapped frantically in an effort to relieve her feelings. Now she was clapping alone. Mr Harkness was frowning at her. Charles was watching her with a little smile. She stopped hastily in confusion.

The minister rose next. He had given pride of place to the priest, because, in the North of Ireland it was important to let everyone see that priests were accorded, if anything, more than their rightful place. In the Free State, in the same type of gathering the minister would have been asked to speak first. Just the Irish mistake of sharpening the compliment to an insult.

Though he had made his gesture with a good grace the minister had no intention of allowing his own speech to be anything but the major event of the proceedings. There was unfortunately, for the listeners, nothing new for him to say. However, undaunted by a detail of this nature, he spoke of Mr John Harkness, of the mill, of the village and of Mr John Harkness. Isobel was fast approaching uncontrollable hysteria. She was certain that in another minute she would laugh aloud. She was weak from the effort of restraint.

Charles rose and tiptoed softly across the room. The minister paused and looked at him reproachfully, but Charles pretended to be engaged in opening a window which was already open. He gave an apologetic smile in the direction of the speaker and sat down beside Isobel, obviously to avoid disturbing the minister by recrossing the room. The slight distraction probably saved Isobel from making an exhibition of herself. She managed to concentrate her thoughts on Charles and his many excellent qualities. Normally, she would have considered this a dangerous line of thought, but under the circumstances anything was safer than hearing the speech. She needed a powerful anodyne for her hysterical exasperation.

The performance was over at last. They did some weird and wonderful conjuring with the vote of thanks, which was proposed by the minister, seconded by the priest, returned to the minister, who, after toying with it for some time threw it to the company. The company obligingly clapped loudly and said, 'Hear! hear!' Mr John Harkness thereupon replied to the vote of thanks, after which he announced that the dancing might proceed until midnight.

Isobel stared at Charles. 'Do you mean to say that it's not midnight yet?'

He put an arm round her. 'Come and dance. You're going to have a nervous breakdown if you don't look out. It's perfectly ridiculous working yourself into a state like that over a few speeches. I'm ashamed of you.'

'I couldn't help it. There ought to be a law against that kind of thing – it's really criminal. I nearly screamed quite a number of times.'

Charles laughed. 'It is pretty awful, I admit. I always go over all the poems I know. I was stuck in "Tintern Abbey" when I noticed you … What comes after, "I have felt a Presence that disturbs me …?"'

'That Presence, ladies and gentlemen, is the mill. It stands for something permanent …' Isobel broke off and giggled inanely. She had every appearance of being slightly drunk.

Charles shook her. 'My father is watching you, Isobel.'

Isobel stiffened. 'Your father's opinion is the least of my worries. He likes people to respect him and obey him and fear him. He does not like to see you dancing with a mill girl so often. He's considering the dignity of the firm, of course. Charles, I hate him. I don't think I ever hated anyone before, but I hate your father.'

Charles led her to the door. 'I think I'll take you home, Isobel. You're tired and overstrung.'

Isobel was glad enough to get away. She knew she had been very foolish. She ought not to have spoken to Charles of his father as she had done. In fact it was stupid to regard John Harkness in such a light. He was probably no more sinister than any other man with an over-exaggerated notion of his own importance.

'I'm sorry,' she said, on the homeward journey, 'that I spoke like that about your father. I did not mean to be personal ... Sometimes I don't regard your father as a person, but just as the spirit of the mill ... it goes on spinning yarn, spinning yarn, spinning yarn. It frightens me.'

'It doesn't matter in the least,' said Charles. 'I know you don't mean what you say. Perhaps you realise now the foolishness of undertaking a job that is beyond you?'

The girl nodded. 'Yes, I shall leave at the end of the month ... if I stayed I'd not only hate your father, but I'd probably fall in love with you.'

The man looked at her with a queer smile. 'That, I presume, is intended to queer the pitch, so to speak. I'm sorry you feel like that but, is it altogether fair to blame me for what is your own purely imaginary view of my father?'

'I don't know what you mean,' said Isobel stonily.

'No? Think it over. I shall not assume denseness. I understand what you mean perfectly. I assure you it was quite unnecessary.'

Isobel shrugged. 'Well, there's no harm done. But I cannot allow you to make me feel small, Charles Harkness ... You see, I cannot afford to feel small. I was not assuming ... anything. I was not warning you. I didn't think that necessary. If there were a warning it was to myself ... Gripping the nettle. I could fall in love with you very easily.'

'And you don't intend to?'

'Oh, no.'

'Because?'

'Because lots. Funny conversation we seem to be having, isn't it? Would you mind, supposing I did? That, of course, is sheer idle curiosity.'

'Very much. It would be embarrassing. That, of course, is sheer self-defence.'

The smile that accompanied and belied his words made Isobel uncomfortably aware of the action of her heart. She swerved the conversation with more speed than skill. 'Charles, why do you let me run on like this? I'm quite mad tonight.'

'Absolutely,' agreed Charles. 'But remember that you have given your word to leave the mill at the end of the month. I shall hold you to that.'

'You won't hold me to the rest?'

'About not falling in love? No. Women are allowed to change their minds. Since you find spinning and listening to speeches so difficult it seems a pity to set your face against something you could do very easily.'

'This is the house,' said Isobel.

'Goodnight, Isobel,' he said with decision. 'Tomorrow you will blame me for every word you say tonight. Sleep on it. When you have made up your mind whether you love me more than you hate my father, I shall do what I can about your wishes.'

For once Isobel had nothing to say.

CHAPTER FIVE

John Harkness's 'Good morning!' to Charles was curt. Certainly Charles was twenty minutes late for breakfast, and John Harkness disliked unpunctuality, but Marie had received a more gracious greeting, and she also had been late.

'Where did you disappear to last night?' demanded Marie, with sisterly curiosity.

'I didn't disappear,' said Charles. 'I got tired of waiting to get past Peter Montgomery to have my duty dance with my beloved sister, so I came away.'

'You came in long after we did. Daddy, I believe Charles has lost his heart at last. Did you notice the girl with the Garbo-looking expression?'

'She hasn't a Garbo-looking expression,' said Charles. 'The speeches made her look like that.'

John Harkness regarded his son with disfavour. 'Do you think it was necessary to dance the entire evening with the same girl?'

Charles helped himself to toast. 'Not necessary. But you don't go to a party to do necessary things.'

His father grunted. 'I suppose you go to a party in order to make yourself conspicuous? You were remarkably successful.'

'Nonsense,' said Charles. 'It's the custom now – specialisation, you know. Peter Montgomery danced all night with Marie, which was much more serious.'

'He didn't,' said Marie, in confusion, which her father was too annoyed to notice. 'He danced ever so many duty dances.'

'That means that those he danced with you were not duty dances. You're making matters worse, Marie,' laughed Charles.

'Marie behaved herself with circumspection,' said John Harkness heavily. 'At a function such as took place last night social distinctions must be ignored – to a certain extent. I am not objecting to your dancing with any of the mill girls, but I think it was rather unfortunate that you showed preference for one in particular.'

'You think the others might take it to heart?' asked Charles flippantly.

'No, I consider that extremely improbable. But they will gossip, and in any case it was no kindness to the girl. Girls of that type are likely to take a wrong view of that kind of thing.'

'She was not a girl "of that type" whatever you mean by that,' replied Charles angrily. 'And I can assure you she knows my intentions perfectly. You can leave her out of the conversation if you don't mind.'

Both men were thoroughly angry. Marie looked a little scared. She was not used to open family differences.

'I shall do nothing of the kind,' snapped John Harkness. 'Your behaviour would have been bad enough, but the whole situation was made worse by the objectionable character of the girl you decided to honour with your intentions.'

Charles went white.

In desperation Marie plunged into the conversation. 'Oh, that's not true, daddy. She is a very nice girl. Peter Montgomery told me she was.'

Charles dropped his fork. Marie glanced at him in surprise, and he cautiously showed her a closed fist. This was a childish innovation of Marie's invention, to be translated literally. 'You are giving me away.'

She looked puzzled, but could not ignore the family sign. 'An exceptionally nice girl,' she amended rapidly, if not very brilliantly. She glanced fearfully at Charles and was considerably relieved by his nod of approval.

John Harkness had already regretted his undignified outburst. He realised that Marie's intervention had spared him a speech from Charles, which both would have regretted.

'I dare say she was merely excited by the party,' he said in a milder tone. 'I don't want to be unduly critical. I appreciate the fact that this party is exceptional. You will pardon me, Marie, I must be getting along.' He rose and left the room.

Marie turned to Charles. 'My goodness! I thought there was going to be a dreadful row. Charles, whatever came over you?'

Charles passed his cup for more tea. 'Nothing. By the way, Marie, I can't say I particularly like Peter Montgomery. You've become very friendly all of a sudden, haven't you?'

Marie made no attempt at a denial. 'Yes, I like him. I've been out with him several times.'

Charles groaned. 'Poor dad! I'm saying nothing, kid. But if you must go on seeing him I should tell dad if I were you, even though there's absolutely nothing in it. Secret meetings are stupid. If you're not ashamed of being friendly with him, and there is no reason why you should, be friendly openly.'

Marie nodded. 'Yes, I'll have to tell him. But I don't want Peter to get the sack on my account. Why didn't you want me to tell dad who Isobel Martin was?'

Charles smiled at her quizzically. 'Just the same story. I didn't want her to get the sack, until she wants to go. But Isobel is very different from young Montgomery.'

'Now you're being a snob,' Marie pointed out.

'No. It's just a matter of common sense, Marie. I do not for one minute think that you have any feelings but those of ordinary friendship for this young clerk. I should be very sorry to think otherwise, not because I think you are any better than he is, but you are used to one kind of life and he is used to another. It would be almost impossible, unless you are both exceptional, to arrange a common life that would suit you both.'

'Anyway, daddy won't approve of Isobel Martin now any more than he will approve of Peter Montgomery,' said Marie crossly.

The auditor was busy with the mill books. John Harkness looked at the clock impatiently. It was not like Mr Grey to be so slow at a comparatively simple and straightforward job. The Head of the Firm made a point of waiting for a personal report, but he also made a point of being punctual for lunch. He looked at the clock again. He was already eight and a half minutes late. Most annoying! There was a discreet knock at the door, and he looked hopeful; but instead of Mr Grey, the new secretary appeared at the door.

'Are you busy, Mr Harkness?' he asked, in his pleasant respectful way.

John Harkness rather liked the lad. 'That you, Montgomery? No, as a matter of fact I am waiting for the auditor's report. Mr Grey is taking his time today.'

Peter Montgomery closed the door quietly. 'In that case perhaps you could spare me a few minutes, sir?'

'Certainly. No trouble I hope?'

Peter Montgomery hesitated. His manner conveyed, as it was intended to convey, a certain measure of reluctance. 'It is rather a difficult point. I have put off speaking to you for some time ... but in the interests of the mill I feel that it is my duty to draw your attention to something ... I should not feel satisfied if I refrained from an obvious duty.'

John Harkness stared. 'Well, Montgomery, what is it?'

'Have you noticed Mr Davidson recently, sir?'

'Davidson? No. What about Davidson? '

'I'm afraid he is insane, Mr Harkness.'

John Harkness jumped. 'My God, boy, what are you saying? Davidson has been with us for years ... Insane! Nonsense, nonsense!'

The young man managed to look very worried. He said nothing.

John Harkness considered the point for a minute in silence, then he turned to his secretary impatiently. 'You must have some grounds for a statement of that nature?'

Peter nodded gravely. 'This is very painful, Mr Harkness ... There have been incidents, very peculiar incidents ... lately they have been more frequent. It may be quite temporary ... I believe that is often the case.'

'Now, Montgomery,' said John Harkness sternly. 'I want the facts. All the facts, if you please. What are these incidents to which you refer?'

'Well, sir, the first time l noticed anything was some six months ago. A representative from one of our best customers called. Mr Davidson was busy and you were not at the mill. I interviewed hiin myself. He showed me a remarkable letter from Mr Davidson, stating that we were not prepared to take any further orders from this particular house. I asked him for the letter.' Peter placed the letter on the desk. 'I said that Mr Davidson had been ill and that I would see to his orders myself ... I did not care to approach you, Mr Davidson being the manager ...'

'Go on.'

'There were several other cases of this nature. I managed to smooth things over, and since then I have attended to that side of the business myself.'

John Harkness nodded. 'I noticed that. And you've done remarkably well.'

'I spoke to Mr Davidson at the time,' continued Peter, 'and he was very odd, very odd indeed.'

'What explanation did he give?'

'He said it was the wish of the Lord ... The Ringawoody Mill had been cursed with seven curses. Sheer nonsense of that kind, sir.'

John Harkness did not move. His face was a mask. 'Anything else?' he asked slowly.

'He took over most of the accounts, and for a time he seemed to be all right. I was very busy and I had not a great deal of time to notice anything. But I heard a good deal of talk. I would rather not repeat what may be exaggerated gossip; you know what the girls are like? Outsiders too, have been remarking on his strangeness in the village. He goes into shops and orders rather wildly – the oddest things – sherbert, umbrellas; lately, he has been bringing in enormous quantities of pens ... I am afraid that he is getting worse.'

John Harkness rose. 'This is bad, Montgomery. You ought to have told me at once. Yes, I quite understand how you felt, especially as a newcomer. Davidson, of all people! He has a wife and family too. I had better see him. Will you kindly ask him to come here, Montgomery?'

'Certainly, Mr Harkness. Do you wish me to be present?'

There was a knock at the door. John Harkness turned. 'This will be Mr Grey ... Come in, Mr Grey. Just one moment, Montgomery ...'

Mr Grey came into the room slowly. He looked puzzled and grave. He placed his report on the desk. 'I am rather late, Mr Harkness, but under the circumstances I considered a recheck was necessary. I shall be glad if you will look into this at once as I wish to be in town by three.'

John Harkness stared at the report in amazement. 'But, Mr Grey! £207 short in the Petty Cash ... There must be some mistake. This has never happened before.'

Mr Grey pursed his lips. 'I am afraid that there is no mistake, Mr Harkness, except perhaps in the book keeping. It is possible that some expenses have not been entered yet.'

John Harkness and Peter Montgomery exchanged glances. Peter looked worried and very sorry, but not surprised.

'Get Mr Davidson, please,' said John Harkness curtly, 'and come back yourself.'

Montgomery withdrew.

Mr Grey sat down and picked up the report. 'This young fellow is the new secretary?'

'Yes, but actually he has been doing Davidson's work. I think that Davidson has been looking after the books.'

'I see. Can you suggest any possible explanation?'

John Harkness nodded. 'I am afraid I can. But wait until we hear what Mr Davidson has to say.'

The accountant frowned. 'As far as I remember, Davidson always looked after the books here. They were exceptionally well kept.'

The door was suddenly thrown open and William Davidson strode in, followed by Peter who looked the picture of misery. Davidson stared at the accountant. 'The Lord is on my side,' he said loudly.

The accountant jumped, recovered himself hastily, and murmured, 'Quite so.'

John Harkness picked up the report, and addressed Davidson sternly. 'Mr Davidson, I see from Mr Grey's report that there is a bad deficit in the Petty Cash. Can you suggest anything to account for this?'

Davidson raised his arm dramatically. 'This mill is cursed, twice, thrice, seven times cursed ... with the great curse and the less. The flax rots, the yarn snaps ... Ringawoody is cursed. The house of Harkness is cursed. The Lord has spoken. I am on the Lord's side!'

Mr Grey sprang to his feet in consternation. 'The man is stark, staring mad,' he said excitedly.

John Harkness played with his fountain pen absently.

'Mr Davidson,' said Peter, quietly, 'there is a little trouble with the books. Try to remember if you bought or ordered anything for the mill which you omitted to enter up.'

'All is entered in the Book of Life,' said Davidson. 'Be not impatient, my children. All will be revealed on the Last Day. Do not fret and weary yourselves with small things. See, I shall pay my little debt.' He put his hand in his pocket and solemnly handed John Harkness fivepence. 'Had I more,' he said sadly, 'you should have it. But I have had many things to provide. The curse must fall, but I have staved off the ill day. We know not what hour it may strike. Be prepared. You, John Harkness, Head of the Firm, Master of Ringawoody, Head of the House of Harkness, be warned. I say to you, bend – bend in the winds of adversity or you will surely break and be utterly overthrown. After the daylight comes the dark.'

John Harkness turned to the accountant. 'Will you write off this sum as a retiring bonus to Mr Davidson. I do not see any point in pursuing enquiries further. Montgomery, will you ring up Dr McDonald. Tell him it is urgent; that I want him to come right along. Then you might wait here with Mr Davidson until the doctor arrives ... I think that once the doctor has seen him you had better take him home, until we have a further opinion. Explain the circumstances to his wife as tactfully as possible ... And, by the way, you will be in charge here until I can make arrangements. I am going to lunch now. Should anything unforeseen arise 'phone me at the house.'

When the two men were gone, Peter turned to Davidson. 'Sit over there at the desk and count those pens.I think one was missing.'

Davidson hastily pulled several large bundles of pens from his pockets and began to count aloud. Peter lifted the phone and rang through to 'Craigaveagh.'

'May I speak to Miss Harkness, please? Yes, it is most important. No, no name.'

Peter waited impatiently until he heard Marie's voice. 'Listen, Marie, I must see you this evening. You have an engagement! You must cancel it. This is urgent. No, I cannot explain over the 'phone. There has been a lot of trouble and your father is very worried. He may tell you; if not, I shall explain. You said on Saturday that you were going to tell him soon about seeing me. You must say nothing today, absolutely nothing. Do you understand? This is no time to worry him, and it might do me a great deal of harm.'

Marie's voice sounded completely bewildered. 'Whatever you say, Peter. But it all sounds very mysterious. Where shall I see you this evening?'

'Take your own car to Downpatrick. I'll meet you outside the Post Office at seven. We can go to Newcastle. Remember, say nothing.'

He rang off and sat down to wait for the doctor while William Davidson counted and recounted his pens.

Peter had purposely arranged his meeting with Marie, in order to give him time to call with his mother. He called at the cottage and was informed by Bessie that Mrs Montgomery was over at Ballycam visiting Nancy. He, therefore, turned his car in the direction of the farm.

Frank Orr's farm was as good as any and better than most of its kind in the county. Even in the bleak, half-dark of a winter afternoon, the fields, despite their desolation, had a well-tended look. The outhouses were in good condition. The solid-looking farmhouse had an air of prosperity and comfort. Peter took in the details with observant eyes. The Orrs were prospering. He certainly had no reason to be ashamed of Nancy. She had done remarkably well for herself. Farmers like the Orrs, while they did not strive after the refinements of education on which folk of the Martin ilk insisted, were nevertheless well thought of and held themselves to be as good as any.

Peter knocked on the kitchen door and entered. Eliza was preparing the men's tea. Whatever might be her shortcomings in Nancy's eyes, she kept the kitchen as spotlessly clean as even her mistress could have wished. The ruddy glow from the range, innocent of black lead, or 'such-like dirt' as Nancy termed it, but scoured to a silvery brightness with constant applications of emery paper and daily washings, lit up a room that might well kindle pride or envy in the breast of any farmer's wife. The table was obtrusive in its almost unnatural cleanness, as was also the red-tiled floor. Brass work gleaming in the firelight spoke of endless industry; pots, pans and delph displayed themselves ostentatiously as testimonials to their owner's thorough grasp of the rules of housewifery. The sweet, satisfying smell of newly-baked bread filled the kitchen.

Eliza was cutting great slices from a wheaten cake. She stared at Peter. 'Was you wanting anything?' she asked.

'Yes,' said Peter. 'I am Mrs Orr's brother. I understand that my mother is here. I should like to see her.'

Eliza lit a small hand lamp, and led the way to the wide stair with its shallow oak steps. 'Mind, and you no slip,' she warned. 'The stairs is polished.' She led Peter down a long passage and threw open the door of Nancy's room. 'Your brother was wanting to see you,' she explained, and promptly vanished down the passage.

Peter entered the room. He had deliberately trained himself to appear at ease with most people and under most conditions. His assumed poise had become so much a part of him that he was incapable of relaxing and being completely off his guard. He was, therefore, most uncomfortable with those for whom his meticulously erected pretences were useless or unnecessary.

Nancy was propped up in the huge bed. She was very pale. Pain and disappointment had etched tiny, temporary lines round her rather hard mouth, but her dark eyes were as bright as ever as she regarded her brother with the old, half-scornful, half-accusing glance. Mrs Montgomery sat by the bedroom fire. She had been engaged in folding minute garments in tissue paper and packing them in an open box which lay on the floor. The sight of her son swept the sentimental pathos from her face.

'Peter!' she cried. 'Oh! But I'm that glad to see you, son.'

Peter Montgomery kissed his mother as a fourteen-year-old schoolboy might kiss an aunt whom he sometimes met at Christmas. As he did so he was unpleasantly aware of his mother's tenderness, his own coldness and his sister's mocking, vindictive eyes. He turned to Nancy with an almost desperate effort at sympathetic kindliness. 'I was very sorry to hear the bad news, Nancy. I hope you are feeling fairly fit.'

'You took a brave bit of time over expressing your sorrow,' said Nancy. 'But I was none the worse of that. I'm grand, thank you, Peter. We were just talking about you ... but surely you never came this length to see me.'

Mrs Montgomery fluttered nervously. 'Nancy, dear, you should no be so bitter. Peter never did you any harm. Why will you no give the lad a bit of peace?'

'He never did me any good either,' said Nancy. 'Nor to any other body either. Peter is over busy being good to himself.'

Peter laughed. 'Do not worry, mother. Nancy is not responsible for her tongue. I wanted to see you about the house. You can move in on the 7th. I have arranged everything. It will be rent free to you, while I am able to pay the rent. I have arranged for a van to come for the furniture. You and the children can go up on the bus. This is the address.' He handed her a slip of paper.

'Where is the grand residence?' asked Nancy.

Mrs Montgomery read proudly from the paper. 'Meadow Street ... Sure it sounds nearly like the country. Peter, the Lord will reward you for your thought for your mother.'

'He will, surely,' said Nancy, looking smilingly at her brother. 'I know Meadow Street, rightly, Peter, off York Street, is it not? A nice quiet spot, select too, and brave and near the cheap shops. Aye, you were thoughtful, Peter – for your own pocket. Where, in the name of God, are you raising the cash for all this grandeur; cars, hotels, and the dear knows what! And now a house for your ma!'

Peter avoided his sister's eye. 'The rent is fairly reasonable,' he said stiffly.

Nancy's eyes narrowed. 'Maybe, Peter. But petrol, at the rate you use it, is no very reasonable. Mind, Peter, or you'll finish up with two feet in the one boot. I've seen them as ganged your gait ere this. I was hearing Mr Davidson is leaving the mill?' She shot out the question accusingly.

Peter looked confused. 'Bad news travels fast,' he said. 'Yes, poor Davidson is finished. You were right enough about him, Nancy. He's quite insane.'

'God help his wife and bairns,' said Mrs Montgomery. ''Tis a bad business, so it is. Though, as I was saying to Mrs Moore, I'm no surprised. 'Twas a disgrace, him manager of the mill and the way he was. 'Tis the great wonder he has no the place ruined.'

Nancy lay back on her pillows. 'I heard there was money gone, Peter, a lot of money. That, maybe, is but gossip. Sure most of the shops laughed at yon man's daft orders; 'twould be easy to reckon if he wasted much that road.'

Peter shrugged. 'Any talk of money missing is pure gossip. People will say anything now that the unfortunate man cannot defend himself.'

'Aye, people are bad,' said Nancy. ''Twould be a cruel wrong to blame an innocent man because he was mad. But there is folks as would do it, Peter. There is folks as would do it.'

Peter Montgomery rose. 'Well, I must be going, Are you coming, mother? I'll run you home.'

'Ma is no going yet,' said Nancy sullenly.

Mrs Montgomery interposed hastily. 'Aye, Nancy. I'm for going with Peter. 'Tis no every night I get a ride in a car – and with my own son, too.' She smiled her admiration of her son as she carefully donned her outdoor clothes. 'Do I look right now, Nancy?' she asked with pathetic earnestness.

'Grand, ma. You're the best looking in the family.' Nancy returned her mother's kiss. 'See it's no long till you're back. Goodnight till you and give my love to the wee lassies.'

Peter opened the door for his mother and turned to Nancy with an outstretched hand. 'See you look after yourself,' he said cheerfully.

Nancy ignored the hand. 'I need no tell yourself that, Peter. But see you dinna draw too much attention to your spending – if your salary is no too big. Whangs from another man's leather are brave and easy to spot.'

Peter looked at her doubtfully, made as though to speak, then changing his mind he followed his mother from the room.

Nancy stared unseeingly at the tiny garments strewn on the floor. 'He's worse than I thought,' she told herself. 'Far, far worse than I thought.'

Chapter Six

Marie Harkness took the Quoile bend badly. Her thoughts were not on her driving. Pulling herself together with an effort she narrowly missed the wall of the bridge and, more by good luck than good judgment, skidded safely round the corner to the strip of road that skirted Jane's Shore.

This particular spot, just outside Downpatrick, was one of Marie's favourite views. Charles used to laugh at her and tell her it was ridiculous to compare it with the view from the Quarter Hill or St John's Lighthouse, in fact any view across Dundrum Bay to the Mourne Mountains. It was too orthodoxly pretty, like a limited, neat view one might see on a picture postcard. But vast sweeps were beyond Marie. She liked this view of Jane's Shore, it reminded her of Tennyson's Island of Shalott. The dark, mysterious woods might well screen an enchanted castle. They actually screened the historic ruins of Inch Abbey, thus Marie was able to fit abbots on ambling pads into the picture very easily. Today, however, Marie's Tennysonian romances were as far away as her enthusiasm for the League of Nations. Reality has a nasty habit of cutting across idealistic imagery. For the frst time in her life Marie Harkness had to face facts.

In Marie's eyes these facts were pleasant enough. She imagined herself very much in love with Peter, and she imagined Peter to be desperately in love with herself. She did not believe that her father would oppose her in this matter to the point of causing her unhappiness. Marie was not in the least afraid of her father. With fierce, youthful aggression she longed to display her loyalty to Peter by facing up to her father's temporary wrath. She resented Peter's caution, and she was growing weary of the elaborate deception to which he forced her. By the time she pulled up outside the Post Office she had fully decided that Peter must be persuaded to tell her father; that they would become openly engaged immediately, and that they must be married next June. She had not quite made up her mind whether to have blue or pink for the bridesmaids.

Peter was already waiting. Marie looked at him sympathetically, and decided that he was over-worked. He looked tired and strained.

'You look all out,' said Marie. 'Shall I drive?'

'No,' said Peter rudely, then hastily. 'That is, if you don't mind.' He smiled his charming smile. 'I hate sitting beside a bad driver.'

Marie slid into the vacant seat in silence. Peter took the wheel, turned sharply left, then right, and sped out past the Railway Station on to the Newcastle road.

Marie held her breath. 'Talk about bad driving!' she gasped. 'That policeman would have stopped you if you'd given him time.'

Peter slackened his speed slightly. 'Sorry. I'm afraid I'm rather on edge. We had a most unpleasant scene at the mill today.'

'Daddy told me about it,' said Marie. 'He's fearfully upset, too. Seems to think it reflects on that silly old mill of his. It's all rather nonsense. I always thought Davidson was a bit off his chump.'

Peter nodded. 'He was always a bit odd certainly. But, Marie, we must be very careful not to arouse your father's suspicions just now. This is a very critical period for me.'

Marie pouted. 'I don't see that. You'll be manager now instead of Davidson, and once daddy gets over the first shock he'll see how very suitable it is ... I think this is the best time to tell him.'

'You know nothing about it,' said Peter sharply. 'If you make trouble now he will merely sack me and bring in new men. I have not been offered Davidson's position. I could hardly expect it with so little experience. My only chance is to take things easy until he decides what to do. For my sake, Marie, you might show a little consideration and patience.'

Had Peter been less taken up with visions of his own future he would have noticed Marie's glance of offended hostility. But the possibility of being manager of Ringawoody Spinning Mill was more important than the necessity to placate Marie Harkness. Peter had no intention of permitting his ambitions to be frustrated by the whim of any girl.

Marie said nothing for some minutes. She was angry and perplexed. For the moment she decided that after all she was not so very much in love with Peter Montgomery. He was not nearly as nice as she had thought. When he was annoyed he became impertinent. Marie had already planned out Peter's role, and it was pure cheek on his part to go on like this. She lit a cigarette and said coldly. 'I don't think I want to go to Newcastle or anywhere else. Will you please turn? I wish to go home.'

Peter swore at her under his breath but outwardly he was all contrition. 'We won't go to Newcastle. I'll take the Hilltown road and we'll go through the mountains. I've been looking forward to this run with you all day, Marie, please, don't be angry with me.'

'Why won't you let me tell daddy?' demanded Marie obstinately. 'Charles says that we cannot go on like this, and he's perfectly right. It's stupid.'

'Did you tell Charles?' asked Peter crossly.

'I told him that I had been out with you. He was not at all pleased.'

'I am quite sure he was not,' said Peter grimly. 'I daresay he will save you the trouble of telling your father. Of all the silly –' Peter checked himself hastily as Marie turned on him in anger.

'Peter, you must not speak like that to me. You need not worry; Charles will not tell my father anything. I told him in confidence, and he would not dream of repeating anything I said. But why are you so frightened of daddy knowing?'

'I'm afraid of losing you altogether, Marie. You are so free from snobbery you do not realise that other people are not as broad-minded as yourself. I love that in you, Marie. It's made anything ... everything possible. Before I knew you, I had no ambition. You changed all that. If you have faith in me I can be anything; even your father will admit that I am worthy of you. But you must give me time, Marie. You must trust me.'

Marie melted completely. 'Oh, Peter, I'm so sorry. I know you are clever, and I am sure you are right ... It's just that I hate all this secrecy ... Oh, Peter, don't try to go up this hill without changing gear. Just listen to the poor car!'

Peter concentrated on the flagging car until they reached the summit of the hill. 'I'll give the engine a few minutes to cool,' he said. 'You can admire the scenery. Did you ever see such a God-forsaken country?'

Winter in its uncompromising thoroughness had swept all traces of mere prettiness from the mountainy country. In the cold, uncertain light of a half-grown moon the dark, heavy bulk of the mountains seemed to glower resentfully on intruders. The kindly Mourne district of June and July had discarded its smile with its summer trappings and permitted itself the relaxation of a frown, but in its gloomy displeasure and desolation it revealed a primitive grandeur scarcely visible in its sunnier moods.

Marie stared at the view with a little shiver. 'It's cold,' she said, 'and lonely and sad, but it's not God-forsaken; some of the most religious people in the world live among these mountains. They walk miles and miles to church on Sunday mornings.'

Peter shrugged. 'Irish peasants go to church regularly for much the same reason as certain English city dwellers attend nightclubs – because they want to get away from the monotony of real life, otherwise they would die of boredom.'

Marie frowned. 'You think any kind of substitute is much the same?'

'I don't think it, I know,' said Peter calmly.

Marie opened the window and breathed the cold, raw air. She was not sure whether she liked it or not. She wrinkled up her face in very much the same way as she had done on attempting to smoke her first cigarette. She finally closed the window and turned to Peter seriously. 'I never can get right through a book that talks like that. I can't see what it's trying to prove, or follow how it's trying to do it. But people who go regularly to nightclubs are always bored, and the people here never seem to be a bit bored, so it looks as if there were some substitutes that don't work at all. I hate people who are always trying to prove that something else is exactly the same thing as something that anyone can easily see is quite different. People like that are so clever that they are afraid of anything obvious, so they invent a different answer, and if it's different it doesn't matter whether it's right or wrong.'

Peter tucked the rug more closely round her and drew her closer. 'If you're going to preach a sermon, you might as well be comfortable. Wake me when you're finished. I want to talk about us.'

'What about us?' demanded Marie curiously.

'What exactly did your brother say when you told him that you had been out with me?' asked Peter unexpectedly.

Marie hesitated. 'I don't think he realised that I was serious.'

'You mean that he did not want to think so?'

Marie nodded. 'Yes, I'm afraid it was like that. But Charles need not talk. He wants to marry Isobel Martin.'

Peter was interested. 'Isobel Martin? Are you sure?'

'Oh, yes, I'm quite sure. Daddy and Charles had a row over her at breakfast the other morning. Daddy was mad because Charles danced with her all night at the Party.'

'Did he say anything about my dancing with you?' asked Peter doubtfully.

'Not daddy. But Charles did. Daddy didn't pay any attention; he was too angry with Charles. Of course he doesn't know who Isobel is. Charles wouldn't let me tell him. I think men are very silly. I'm quite sure daddy wouldn't have been nearly so cross if he had known.'

'But I'm very much afraid that he would be exceedingly cross with me for giving her a job in his mill,' said Peter. 'I wish I had taken nothing to do with it. It seems to me, Marie, that your father is going to have quite a lot of trouble soon. You and I had better save up our bomb until times are quieter. I want you to promise me not to say one word to your father about me until I am safely established as manager.'

'But you might not be made manager at all,' Marie pointed out. 'You could never tell what daddy might do.'

'Leave that to me,' said Peter. 'It may take time but I'll manage it sooner or later, if you back me up. Have I your promise, Marie?'

'Very well,' said Marie. 'I won't say anything.'

Margaret and Edward Harkness were dressing for dinner two weeks after the tragic retirement of William Davidson.

'I wonder why your father invited us tonight?' said Margaret. 'This is not our night for dining at "Craigaveagh", and your father is usually so very regular in his routine.'

'I expect he wants to tell me what he's going to do about this fix at the mill. I hope he's not going to suggest making that lad Montgomery manager.'

Margaret brushed her hair thoughtfully. 'It must be very dull for you – just to be told what your father's going to do. Does it ever strike him that you're nearly forty, not fourteen, Edward?'

Edward attempted a laugh. His wife seldom interfered, but when she did so her remarks were usually to the point, and this was a very sore one with Edward. 'To be perfectly candid, Margaret, I don't believe it does. I feel a pretty useless passenger in the firm sometimes. Charles must feel the same. As a matter of fact I strongly suspect that there will be a bust-up one of these days where Charles is concerned.'

Margaret regarded her husband speculatively. 'It's ridiculous, Edward, and exceedingly humiliating. By the way, did you have a 'phone call from father today?'

'From your father? Yes. I forgot to mention it. He wants me to have lunch with him on Tuesday.'

'He did not say anything more?' asked Margaret.

'He said something about a proposition. You look as if you know all about it?'

Margaret nodded gravely. 'I do, Edward. Father is going to ask you to be a partner in the Mountport Linen Mill. Senior Partner. He will retire if you accept. It's just as well to have time to think about it. Father is inclined to be somewhat impetuous once he has set his heart on anything.'

The usually placid Edward was stirred to something closely resembling excitement. 'But Margaret, that's wonderful. I had no idea that he was entertaining such a scheme.'

'He has no son,' Margaret said. 'His son-in-law is better than an outsider, and you must remember that our three small sons are his grandsons. Father always looks generations ahead.'

'I shall think it over,' said Edward, trying to convince himself that he had not already fully made up his mind. 'It's a big step. I must mention it to dad tonight.'

'I do not see that he can make the slightest complaint,' said Margaret evenly. 'He obviously has no use for your services himself. It is almost criminal that a man of your organising ability should waste the best years of your life listening to statements of what your father has decided to do. Besides, at the best Charles will always have equal control as far as Ringawoody is concerned. You will be definitely able to show what you can do at Mountport, which, incidentally, is a much larger mill.'

'I should say it is!' agreed Edward. 'And I hardly think dad will worry – except perhaps for sentimental reasons – if it were not for the question of transfer of capital. He won't like that.'

'That's nonsense,' said Margaret briskly. 'You obviously must be a shareholder in Mountport. Edward, you must not allow him to stand in your light. I don't want to sound selfish, but I think we have put up with this state of affairs quite long enough. Had your father needed you it would have been different, but he doesn't. He merely regards you as a sleeping partner to whom he can tell his plans. I shall be most disappointed in you, Edward, if you refuse.'

Edward said nothing. He would do a good deal to avoid disappointing his wife; and, in this particular instance he considered that she would have every reason to regard him as a perfect fool if he refused. Edward had no intention of refusing. Whatever he may or may not have been he was no fool.

Charles was not present at dinner.

'He's taking his best girl out to supper,' said Marie blithely, in reply to Edward's query as to his absence.

'I did not know that he had a best girl,' said Margaret with interest. 'Who is she?'

Marie smiled at her father. 'Daddy does not approve of her, so we don't mention her much. She works in the mill.'

Edward almost choked. 'In the mill!' he spluttered.

John Harkness glowered. 'Are you inferring that your brother is carrying on an affair with that person he danced with at the Party?' he asked Marie coldly.

'She's not a person,' said Marie, stoutly defending her favourite brother's choice. 'She's a very nice girl, and Charles is very much in love with her.'

Margaret Harkness laughed. 'Marie is being hopefully romantic, father. I don't think I quite see Charles marrying a mill girl. Charles always strikes me as being the most fastidious member of the family.'

'So he is,' agreed Marie. 'But you haven't seen his mill girl.'

'Marie, be quiet!' said John Harkness with severity. 'We are not interested in your nonsense.'

Marie subsided, and the rest of the meal was distinctly flat. Margaret and Marie were both glad to escape in order to have the opportunity of continuing the exceedingly interesting topic of Charles's love affair in the privacy of the drawing room.

When the ladies had withdrawn, Edward broached the subject of his father-in-law's proposition with a certain amount of diffidence. John Harkness listened in silence.

'You wish to accept?' he asked at length.

Edward looked uncomfortable. 'If you have no serious objection, I do. It is a splendid opportunity. I feel that I am pulling very little weight as far as Ringawoody is concerned. It's a bit futile, dad, for a man of my age. I realise of course, that the withdrawal of capital just now is a bit awkward ...'

'You have a perfect right to invest your own money where you please,' said John Harkness with apparent indifference. No mere spectator could guess that his words served as a cloak to hide his shocked disappointment.

For the moment John Harkness was too deeply shaken to be able to find relief in his customary ready anger. From a business point of view he realised that Edward was acting with wisdom, but John Harkness had all the confirmed business man's repugnance to the intrusion of business considerations within those confines where he considered they had no place. Old Norton was a business rival who had beaten him at his own game more often than he cared to remember. Edward was his son, a shareholder in Ringawoody, one of its directors. True, he had never encouraged or permitted him to do any real directing, but the new generation knew nothing about spinning or business. They would not even buy the old-fashioned linen nowadays; you could only persuade them to purchase by painting it to look like gingham or overlaying it with artificial silk to look like nothing on earth. The old substantial standards were gone. People no longer wanted tablecloths guaranteed for a lifetime. They preferred scraps of coloured paper. Marie would sometimes apologise to guests for the valuable damask dinner cloth. 'We're in the linen business, you know, so we have to pretend to like it.'

Norton's were taking up the new fancy schemes and making them pay ... cheap, shoddy changes pandering to the inconstancy of the age. And now his son Edward was going over to the enemy. His three grandsons would never serve their time in Ringawoody. Something of fear tinctured the old man's bitter frustration. The settled, permanent future of the firm of Harkness, Harkness and Harkness was no longer assured. He had always felt that he could rely on Edward; Charles had ever been an uncertain proposition.

Edward was relieved by his father's absence of violence. He determined to close the matter as quickly as possible. 'It is very decent of you to take it so well,' he said cheerfully. 'I was afraid that you might be a little prejudiced.'

'When do you propose – making the change?' asked his father.

'There's no immediate hurry. Norton will hang on until I am able to take over.'

'Norton intends to resign?' said John Harkness slowly.

'Yes, at least so Margaret says. I have not spoken to him yet. I thought I would mention it to you first.'

'I see. Well, I wish you luck, Edward. I shall see to the matter of capital this week. I'm afraid it means a mortgage. Textile shares are not easily sold at the present time – even if I were willing to bring in an outside partner, which I am not.'

'No?' Edward's voice was slightly amused. 'Well, I leave it to you to arrange as you think best. Norton will not be unreasonable. He knows that Ringawoody has been doing badly.'

'Ringawoody has been doing better than most spinning mills,' said John Harkness harshly. 'We shall not require to make any demands on Mr Norton's consideration.'

Edward shrugged and changed the subject. 'Did you want to see me about anything tonight?'

John Harkness smiled, a rather twisted smile. 'As a matter of fact I was about to make a demand on some of your superfluous time. We have no manager at the moment. I was going to suggest that you might take the job over until Montgomery had a little more experience.'

Edward frowned. 'If this had not cropped up, I would have welcomed the opportunity of having something definite to do. I should have been quite pleased to take the job over permanently; but I do not approve of the suggestion that Montgomery should ultimately be appointed. He is much too young, has absolutely no training or experience worth mentioning, and personally I don't like him.'

'It's hardly a case for personal prejudices,' said John Harkness drily.

'What about Charles?' said Edward. 'He would be all the better for having a settled interest. He's always messing about the mill looking for something to do. Everybody is saving on wage bills these days.'

John Harkness considered the matter for a minute. 'As a permanent arrangement I am not inclined to approve of the idea. However, I shall speak to Charles.'

'I am sure he would be keen,' said Edward. 'By the way, is there anything in all this chatter of Marie's?'

'For Charles's sake, I hope not,' said John Harkness. 'I have put up with a good deal from Charles, but there are limits to my patience. However, I imagine he has sense enough to realise that.'

Edward looked at his father doubtfully. 'It is, of course, no business of mine,' he said, 'but I should be sorry to see any ill-feeling arise between you and Charles, especially as things have turned out. I think it would be wise to ignore the matter as long as possible and avoid forcing an issue.'

John Harkness rose. 'Shall we join the ladies?' he asked politely.

CHAPTER SEVEN

Marie's guess with regard to Charles's absence from dinner was not far wrong. Being a mill girl did not agree with Isobel Martin, mentally or physically. For a week after the Mill Party she managed to keep going, and, if the spinning master found her more useless than the usual beginner, he made no complaint, partly from a naturally kindly disposition and partly from policy. All the workers were fully aware by this time that Isobel Martin was a favourite with the youngest director.

During the week Isobel took every precaution to avoid Charles, and was naturally furiously indignant with him when she discovered that this was easy. Sometimes she pulled herself up sharply and gave herself a sound lecture. Normally, Isobel was a straightforward, sensible girl. She knew that she was stupidly fond of Charles Harkness. She also knew that John Harkness would not welcome her as a daughter-in-law. There was no sense in shutting her eyes and hoping things would turn out all right, she told herself. She could not reasonably expect Charles to risk a break with his father on her account. The sooner she made up her mind to forget him the better for all concerned.

Having come to this very reasonable conclusion Isobel sensibly sobbed herself to sleep. She woke up with a high temperature and a bad attack of something, which the doctor, for the want of a more definite title, described as influenza. Under the weakening influence of a diet of milk and barley water, Isobel became completely resigned to a sad and lonely life. She hoped that Charles would be lonely too, and also slightly sad. Then, as her temperature abated she began to feel hungry and not nearly so acquiescent. Strangely enough her first sound breakfast coincided with a letter from Charles. Isobel decided that the resignation business was a symptom of infuenza to be discarded with a watery diet. She immediately assured her aunt that she was quite well enough to get up.

Mrs Martin shook her head despondently and talked of complications, but, knowing Isobel, she lit a fire in the back parlour and collected all the cushions in the house on to one armchair. When Isobel finally did make a languid appearance she had considerable difficulty in making room for herself in the chair. A restful day in the back parlour was inclined to be dull. Isobel had just finished *A Tale of Two Cities* when Charles arrived. He could not have arrived at a more opportune moment.

'You shouldn't have come,' she said brightening considerably. 'But just now I'm glad to see anyone.'

'How are you?' asked Charles. 'Your uncle told me to come right in.'

'I am very well, thank you,' said Isobel. 'It is very kind of you to call.'

'Not at all,' said Charles. 'The pleasure is entirely mine. Now I think it's your turn for a remark.'

Isobel moved her hands with an odd little gesture of despair. 'I'm too tired to be witty, Charles. Terrible, isn't it?'

'As bad as that?' he asked. 'What's wrong?'

'Everything.' Isobel impatiently scattered half her cushions on the floor.

Charles collected them and sat beside her on the rug. 'Well, go on,' he prompted. 'What do you mean by "everything"?'

'Oh, I don't know. I'm fed up and miserable.'

'I know,' said Charles. 'It's that mill. I warned you.'

'It's not the mill,' said Isobel crossly. 'It's you.'

Charles took her hand and produced a ring from his pocket. 'It fits jolly well for a guess,' he said, admiring the diamonds flashing on a very unsteady hand. He turned to her with a smile. 'Now you needn't say "This is so sudden!" because that's been said before, and you've been so original up to this it would be a shame to bring down your standard. Besides, you've done all the proposing yourself.'

Charles was gratified to observe that this last remark dispelled her inclination to tears. He rested his head on her knee and listened to the storm. Isobel used up her breath before she exhausted her indignation. She trailed off into a tempestuous silence.

'Now I suppose you'll cry after all,' said Charles mildly.

Isobel laughed. 'You are a silly idiot,' she said softly.

Charles interpreted this as the endearment for which it was intended, but the practical Isobel expostulated. 'You'll take the 'flu off me, Charles, if you kiss me.'

Charles ignored the warning. 'You never had 'flu,' he informed her. 'You just had a heart attack because you were afraid that I was not going to accept your proposal.'

'That's just where you're wrong,' said Isobel. 'Do you think I'd propose to anyone if there was the slightest chance of his daring to refuse me?'

'Somebody once said that the charm of the Irish girl lay in her humility towards her menfolk; she had the sense to accept without question the superiority of Adam, and Eve's comparative insignificance,' said Charles.

Isobel laughed merrily. 'I am sure it wasn't an Irishman said that. Foreigners are easily gulled.'

'Whoever said it knew mighty little about the subject,' agreed Charles. 'When are you coming to be introduced to the family?'

Fear banished the laughter from Isobel's eyes. 'Not yet, Charles. Let's wait.'

'For what?'

Isobel sought desperately for a suitable excuse. 'I'd rather wait until I've finished at the mill.'

'But there's no sense in your going back there. In the first place you're not well enough ...'

'And in the second place?' inquired Isobel.

'I don't like you to be there.'

Isobel stroked his hair coaxingly. 'It won't be for long, Charles. I told my uncle that I was leaving at the end of the month, and I'd rather see it out. I'd hate to let that old mill beat me.'

Charles looked at her thoughtfully. 'I believe you are merely putting off an interview with my father. It must be faced, you know, Isobel.'

She clung to him trembling. 'I know, I know. But don't talk about it now, Charles.'

'Have it your own way,' said Charles. 'I think I'll ask your aunt if we could have some supper. Shall I say you sent me?'

'No. Tell her you're hungry yourself. Auntie loves hungry multitudes. It's a pity ...'

Isobel broke off and Charles paused at the door.

'What's a pity?' he enquired.

'Oh, nothing,' said Isobel. 'I was just thinking.'

Charles Harkness took over the management of Ringawoody the following week. Edward mentioned the subject first, making his own change an excuse for giving Charles a few hints. 'This really clears the ground for you, Charles,' he pointed out. 'And I rather think that when dad gets used to the idea he will be relieved rather than otherwise. But if I were you I should try to avoid annoying him just now. He's had quite a spot of bother one way and another.'

'Just what do you mean by that?' asked Charles smiling.

Edward hesitated. 'Well, he's heard some talk about one of the mill girls.'

Charles's air of innocence was somewhat overdone. 'Terrible!' he said. 'And dad is so particular about his mill girls. Has someone been swearing again?'

'No,' said Edward drily. 'That is not the difficulty this time. However, you know your own business best, but if you take my advice you will bear in mind that dad is not in one of his most reasonable frames of mind at present.'

'Hardly the time to announce an engagement so to speak?'

Edward looked startled. 'Is there an engagement?'

Charles nodded. 'Yes. By the way, Edward, I should like you and Margaret to invite us over one day this week ... Would Tuesday suit you?'

'Who is "us"?' asked Edward cautiously.

Charles made a note on an envelope. 'This is Isobel's address. You remember Hugh Martin of the Knoll? Isobel is his eldest daughter. She's staying with her uncle in Dromara. Margaret might write a note to her.'

Edward's face cleared. 'But of course she will. I remember Isobel quite well ... This is splendid news, Charles. Allow me to congratulate you. Dad will be delighted.'

Charles raised his eyebrows. 'I thought you were trying to give me the tip not to inform him.'

Edward laughed heartily. 'Well, as a matter of fact, the story to which I referred was providing you with a different bride.'

'Indeed,' said Charles, with interest. 'Who was the bride?'

'I don't know that I ever heard her name, but she was one of the mill girls – the one you danced with at the Party.'

'Isobel is working in the mill at present,' said Charles. 'She is also the girl I danced with at the Party. The story is fairly correct after all.'

Edward regarded his brother incredulously. 'You damn fool!' he exclaimed politely. 'You allowed the girl to whom you are engaged take a job like that?'

'I was not engaged to her at the time, and in any case Isobel is not quite the type one allows to do things. Old Martin left nothing but debts, and Isobel was determined to find a job. She tried to get Nancy Orr to take her as a maid, but Frank wouldn't have her because she was Hugh Martin's daughter. It seemed hard lines that the neighbours' high opinion of her family was to prevent the girl from earning a living. I wasn't keen on the idea, naturally, but I could hardly offer her thirty shillings a week to stay at home and save me feeling uncomfortable, so there was nothing else for it. She had been taken on before I found out.'

Edward looked glum. 'Well, get her out of it as soon as you can. You need not mention it at home until she's left.'

'I'll get her out of it as soon as she'll go,' corrected Charles. 'In the meantime she is much more unwilling to have the news broken to dad than he could possibly be to hear it. She's scared stiff of him.'

'It's a good job she's scared of someone,' said Edward with an effort at humour. 'She sounds a bit of a madam. I expect it will be all right. Dad needn't know she's ever been in the mill. She wouldn't have been if he'd known who she was.'

'Or, I suppose, if you'd known?' said Charles grinning.

Edward shrugged. 'Well, never mind. It can't be helped now. I really wanted to see you about something else. Dad is thinking of making you manager. He has a notion of a temporary arrangement until that youth Montgomery serves his time outside the office. But I'd sit on that if I were you. I don't know why, but I don't trust Peter Montgomery. He's too sweet to be wholesome.'

'And thereby hangs another tale,' said Charles. 'Marie has developed a soft spot, I think it's in the head not the heart, for Montgomery.'

Edward looked a bit like a thirsty cod fish.

Charles laughed. 'I wouldn't take it too much to heart, old chap. Marie gets over her fads safely enough. I'll see that Montgomery is kept in his place. I'm quite keen on the manager scheme. It's one of the soundest ideas dad's had for a long time.'

The settlement of the management problem by the appointment of young Mr Charles Harkness was regarded favourably by the entire mill. There had been some little uneasiness lest the job should fall to Montgomery. The workers had their own idea of the fitness of things, and they had a double grudge against the young secretary. They regarded him as being no better than themselves, and hated him for the grand airs with which he tried to cloak this fact. There was, therefore, a general sigh of relief when Charles took over.

At first Peter Montgomery himself shared in the feeling of relief. He decided that Charles Harkness's advent was temporary, and seemed to indicate that his, Peter's, promotion was not too far distant. He began by trying to ingratiate himself with the new manager, but when it became apparent that neither his servility nor his friendliness made any impression on Charles he became guardedly hostile.

A few days after Charles's appointment Isobel Martin gave in her notice. John Harkness insisted on interviewing people who gave in notice unexpectedly. He considered this a satisfactory method of preventing unfair dismissals. Isobel was, accordingly, summoned. Peter was alone in the office with John Harkness when her case came up. He realised that he had been provided with a very timely weapon of offence. He produced Isobel's insurance card and approached John Harkness's desk.

'Before you interview this girl Martin, Mr Harkness, I'd, er – like to suggest that you, er – refrain from inquiring too closely into her reasons for leaving. I think it would be better, under the circumstances, not to encourage her to say too much.'

John Harkness glared angrily. 'Indeed, Montgomery. And why, may I ask, do you offer such extraordinary advice?'

Peter stammered convincingly and muttered 'I beg your pardon, sir.'

'I should think you do,' snapped John Harkness. 'What in God's name are you thinking about, man? If the girl has a grievance I want to hear about it. Think I'm going to have anything hushed up in my mill?'

'No, sir. Of course not, sir.'

'Well, what do you mean by standing there stammering like a half-wit?'

'If you don't mind, sir, I'd rather not say anything.'

John Harkness threw the insurance card from him in fury. 'You'd "rather not say" sir? What would you rather not say?'

Peter looked abjectly miserable. 'I merely wished to avoid unpleasantness, Mr Harkness.'

John Harkness's exasperation was increasing steadily. 'If you wish to avoid dismissal you'll endeavour to be a little more intelligible.'

Peter gave every appearance of making a considerable effort. 'This girl who is leaving was friendly with Mr Charles. He danced with her a good deal at the Party. I think that it is quite possible that he has realised that there has been a certain amount of gossip and has probably dismissed her.'

John Harkness grew calmer. 'But she has not been dismissed, I understand.'

'Quite so, sir. That is why I suggested ...'

'I see. That will do, Montgomery. In future you might mind your own business. You may go.'

Peter departed outwardly crestfallen, but inwardly jubilant. He had not exactly expected John Harkness to clap him on the shoulder and say, 'Thank you, my boy. I appreciate your good intentions.' But despite Mr Harkness's wrath he had a shrewd idea that he had done himself no harm; and what was even better in his scheme of things, he had done Mr Charles no good. In the not too distant future Mr Charles Harkness would discover that he had under-estimated Peter's intelligence. On the whole, Peter was thoroughly satisfied with himself. Getting on was simply a matter of intelligent concentration.

John Harkness considered Montgomery' information as he waited for Isobel to make her appearance. While he resented Montgomery's impertinence, he was just as pleased to be in possession of the facts; and, undoubtedly the young fellow meant well, inexperienced and tactless, but a sound fellow, with the interests of the firm at heart. That kind of thing was too rare nowadays. Young people thought only of watching the clock and getting away.

He found himself looking forward to the girl's arrival with curiosity. He had not really looked at her on the night of the Party. His annoyance with Charles had occupied his entire attention. Judging from Montgomery's remarks the two had been fairly friendly. There must be something unusual about the girl if Charles had gone out of his way to be friendly with her. He was far from being the good-natured type of young man who was prepared to be attracted by anyone and everyone. Marie, too, had insisted that the girl was out of the ordinary. John Harkness knew his son much too well to believe for one minute that he had anything to do with the girl's dismissal. In his own peculiar way he sincerely admired those aspects of his younger son's character which he considered most foolish. The suggestion that Charles would dismiss one of the girls from policy annoyed him extremely.

At the moment he felt quite kindly disposed to this unknown young woman whom his son had liked. Unfortunately, the young woman did not know this, and it would be an exaggeration to state that she felt kindly disposed to him.

Isobel knocked and entered the room with that little touch of bravado that is so useful for covering genuine panic. Isobel had foolishly allowed John Harkness to become her pet nightmare. 'I was told to report to you,' she said quickly. 'I am leaving at the end of the month.'

John Harkness looked at her with interest. She was certainly pretty and she spoke well. It was surprising that she was in the mill at all. 'You are leaving of your free will?' he asked.

She nodded. 'Yes.'

He glanced at her card. 'You have not been with us very long?'

'No.'

'You did not care for the work?' he persisted.

'Not particularly.'

John Harkness reflected, not without satisfaction, that Montgomery had been far out in his surmises. This girl had no intention of embarking on any tale of woe. On the contrary, she looked as if she were anxious to get away as quickly as possible. John Harkness was a perverse man. He had fully intended dismissing the girl with a few routine questions. Had she shown the least inclination to be communicative, he would have done so. He nodded towards a chair. 'Sit down a moment, I should like to have a chat with you. I am glad you are leaving. The work obviously does not suit you, and if I could be of any assistance in finding you a more congenial position I should be very pleased to do anything I could.'

Isobel did not sit down. She hardly heard what he was saying except that he was glad she was leaving. The hideous machinery of the place seems to close in on her, and all its terrifying unreality seemed to her to be impersonated in the white-haired man before her. 'I am glad to be leaving too,' she said fiercely. 'I hate this place. It's horrible, horrible!'

John Harkness lit a cigarette. 'You're not used to it, that's all that's wrong,' he said reasonably. 'Some people can never become accustomed to the routine. We once had a girl who became hysterical regularly. Question of nerves.'

'May I go, please?' said Isobel almost desperately.

John Harkness looked at her in surprise. 'But of course, you may go.'

Isobel turned swiftly to the door, and at that moment Charles entered. He glanced from Isobel's white strained face to his father. 'What's wrong, Isobel?' he asked.

'Nothing,' she said urgently. 'I've been seeing Mr Harkness about leaving.'

'The farewell seems to have taken a lot out of you,' said Charles. 'Father, I think we'll send her home now and take her notice for granted. She's been an appalling nuisance right along.'

'I think that is quite a good idea,' agreed John Harkness. 'I am afraid this young lady does not like us very much. She has just been describing the mill as horrible.'

'It is horrible,' said Isobel. 'And you needn't be a bit afraid ... I'm very glad to go, and I hope I shall never see any of you again.' Isobel rushed past Charles and disappeared.

John Harkness looked at his son with a smile. 'I am afraid your friend is not very well.'

' She's not,' said Charles gloomily. 'This place has played havoc with her. What did you think of her?'

'She didn't give me much chance to think anything of her. I've no use for these highly-strung misses,' said his father carelessly.

'But Isobel isn't highly-strung,' said Charles eagerly. 'She's fearfully sane and sensible. I'm sure you would like her if you knew her properly.'

'Perhaps,' said John Harkness drily. 'I quite agree that she's not the ordinary type we get in here. I'm afraid I was rather severe about the Party. But, Charles, you are manager here now. Isobel –' he smiled an unusually humorous smile for John Harkness – 'is leaving, and we'll forget about her, but no more of these friendships. There's nothing wrong with the girl. As a matter of fact, I quite liked her, but the principle of the thing is wrong.'

'Absolutely,' agreed Charles. 'You know, dad, I haven't put in a comfortable hour since that girl came here.'

John Harkness regarded his son thoughtfully. 'In that case it's a good job she's gone. Did you persuade her to leave?'

'Of course,' said Charles. 'I've been trying to persuade her to leave ever since she came.'

John Harkness rose. 'Are you by any chance trying to give me to understand that this girl means anything to you, Charles?'

Charles met his eyes squarely. 'Yes. I'm going to marry her,' he said quietly.

'Not as manager of this mill, or as one of its directors,' said John Harkness.

'In that case I must look for another job,' said Charles. 'By the way, have you the draft of that estimate for Moran's?'

John Harkness produced it. The two men checked the figures. Isobel Martin would have been resentful had she known with what speed and apparent carelessness she had been brushed aside.

'I did not give this particular contract much attention,' said John Harkness. 'Mountport have beaten us there for five years.'

Charles pocketed the draft. 'They won't beat us this year, you can take it from me. Edward knows those figures backwards. It stands to reason Mountport will submit figures as high as they dare, which will mean just getting under these. We can cut on these, and we're going to do so. Morans were good customers.'

John Harkness's face brightened. 'If you beat Mountport on the Moran contract I'll double your salary – even if we lose on the deal.'

'That's a bargain,' said Charles. 'We'll beat Mountport and we won't lose on the deal. I'll be needing more girls by the end of the month.'

'Get ahead with it,' said John Harkness approvingly. 'But keep me informed.'

Considerably later in the day Charles remembered that he had not made the best of his father's moderately friendly attitude to Isobel. He had completely forgotten the trump card of what County Down would describe as her 'decent father.' Charles was rather sorry. He realised that before his ultimatum his father in a more than usually human moment might have permitted the father's decency to outweigh the daughter's crime of earning a living in the only respectable way she could find. But the ultimatum had been delivered. Charles had had plenty of experience of his father's methods. John Harkness would have no hesitation in parting with an offending eye. He would have even less hesitation in cutting off a comparatively unoffending nose to spite his own face.

The winter passed more prosperously than usual in Ringawoody. The price of yarn was improving slightly. The mill, under Charles's enthusiastic management, was doing better than it had done for several years. Moran's order was recaptured together with a number of smaller ones from previous customers who had been attracted away by Mountport's lower prices. Charles made no secret of his engagement to Isobel Martin. Most people agreed that the arrangement was very suitable, though a few disappointed young ladies stated that Isobel Martin knew what she was about all right, and that that scheme of working in the mill, by the way, was just a trick to obtain the attention she would never have received had she taken her chance fairly in honest-to-goodness competition with these same young ladies.

Nancy Orr, who as a sympathetic young matron came in for a number of these confidences, was reported to have informed Jessie Hamilton that a little brains was worth a lot of dowry on the modern marriage market. If she actually said this, which is very doubtful, for Jessie continued to visit with Nancy, she probably intended the compliment more for herself than for Isobel Martin. Nancy liked the boomerang type of compliment.

All the local houses of any size gave parties for the newly-engaged couple except 'Craigaveagh.' John Harkness ignored the whole affair. Nobody mentioned the engagement to him. It was taken for granted that the Head of the Firm did not approve; and even his closest friends did not discuss, within John Harkness's hearing, anything of which he did not approve.

Early in February, a circumstance occurred which aroused a certain amount of interest and not a little ill-will. David Martin's farm in Dromara had been in the hands of the bank for some time. Martin's eviction was merely a matter of securing a purchaser. It was generally expected that the bank would put up the farm for auction in March, and a number of Protestant farmers, including Frank Orr, had talked vaguely of making an effort to boycott the auction and buy the farm at a low figure on Isobel's behalf. Her father had lent a hand many a time to neighbours pressed by high rates and taxes and hard times, and County Down folk have as long a memory for a good turn as a bad one.

The Catholic farmers, approached by Joe O'Kelly, whose farm marched Ballycam and who had been a lifelong friend and neighbour of Frank's, reluctantly agreed to hold off, though many of them had entertained high hopes of a bargain when the farm would come under the hammer. Greed for land is deeply rooted in the being of the true Northern farmer. It was a neighbourly act of no mean significance that they agreed to leave the farm in Protestant hands when they possessed the money to buy them out.

While this scheme was still in its infancy the story got afoot that a private purchaser had approached the bank. At first this was discredited, but it turned out to be true enough. The would-be purchaser, a Michael Fitzpatrick, from the mountains, openly announced in a public house in Castlewellan that he had offered £1,200 for David Martin's place, and that the bank were seriously considering closing the sale privately. At a generous estimate the farm was certainly worth no more than £1,500. This kind of bidding put an end to the local scheme. The Protestant farmers were angry, and there were many comments on Papist treachery. The old catchwords went the rounds. 'Trust them ones to play a dirty trick.' And again. 'We've too straight for the likes of them. They'll buy us out – lock, stock and barrel.'

Catholic public opinion, resenting these remarks somewhat, veered round. Why shouldn't Michael Fitzpatrick buy if he had the money? A Catholic had as much right to the farm as a Protestant, and far more. The Fitzpatricks were in the mountains before a Martin was heard tell of. A Protestant wouldn't give a Catholic daylight if he could get one of his ill-wishing prayers through to the Almighty. Sure, didn't everybody know that yon Craigavon would close the Catholic Schools only for he was afraid of de Valera. The Protestants were that grand in themselves in the North they thought ten Protestant shillings should be worth twenty Catholic ones. They'd have the quare awakening one of these days when they'd wake up and find the Border blown down overnight.

The wiser element on both sides held their tongues and smiled a little. But there were plenty to chatter and several stones were thrown at an Orange drum in Ballynahinch. The Protestants made a good deal of this 'outrage' because the Chapel stoning episode was still being aired with appropriate additions and subtractions.

Michael Fitzpatrick and the Martin farm were completely forgotten in the argument that ensued until David Martin received an intimation from the bank that a purchaser, who wished to remain anonymous, had purchased the farm on behalf of the children of the late Hugh Martin of the Knoll, Downpatrick. Michael Fitzpatrick swore lustily, and said he was well quit of a farm that wouldn't rear good goats. The Catholic farmers shrugged and suggested that there was more than one could go behind backs. Frank Orr and his followers heaved a sigh of relief, but looked puzzled.

The Martins were inclined to suspect Charles Harkness. Isobel immediately tackled him on the subject, but to her surprise he obviously knew nothing about it. Various improbable theories were put forward, but in time the Martins accepted the mysterious stroke of good fortune. Tessie and Bridgit were brought home, and the Martins again held their heads as high as they ever did.

On the last Monday in February the County Down Stag Hounds met at the Spa. Marie Harkness had recovered from her anti-stag hunting fever, though she still insisted that the stag could not possibly enjoy the hunt as much as the hunters pretended to believe. Despite her conscience she was unable to resist the excitement, and she required very little persuasion from Charles to accompany him.

Marie was not a good horsewoman. When Isobel and Tessie appeared Charles suggested that Tessie and Marie might follow at their leisure, and he and Isobel, who were both excellent riders, were soon out of sight. Marie accepted the arrangement thankfully. She knew that her rate of progress bored Charles, and she liked to take her own time. Tessie was a novice and was quite content to jog along beside her.

The hunt proved unfortunate. The first stag refused to run. He had made tracks for the nearest water, and defied the whole pack to dislodge him. One dog was knocked out and another almost blinded before the hounds were driven off. The stag then tossed his head at his tormentors and made his way leisurely back to the demesne. A second stag was loosed. He was an old hand at the game and usually provided a good hunt, but on this particular day he was evidently averse to a long straight run. He headed direct for Ballynahinch where he sought refuge in a grocer's shop. A fair amount of damage was done there, which the grocer, naturally enough, fully detailed in his subsequent account to the Master of the County Down Stag Hounds. After considerable delay the stag was started off again. He next made for the Seaforde road, and was finally headed through the fields in the direction of Ballycam. The going here was good, but the stag was exhausted by his early adventures in Ballynahinch and was evidently flagging.

Isobel and Charles were well to the front, but the hounds were leading, and, for one horrible minute, it looked as if they would get him down in the open stretch before Orr's house.

'Charles, can't you do something?' gasped Isobel.

Charles shook his head. 'The huntsmen will keep the dogs off even if they do catch him. Don't worry.'

'They won't be in time,' said Isobel.

Actually Charles suspected that she was right. Isobel slowed up. 'Go on, if you like. I couldn't watch it. I saw a stag pulled to pieces four years ago at Ardglass. It was dreadful.'

Charles kept on, more from a despairing hope that he might be of use rather than any desire to see the stag being taken. The stag, however, had no intention of being taken. He realised the danger of the open field, and suddenly veered sharply into a lane and made for the back of the farm. Panting wildly, with eyes incredibly distended, the desperate animal charged into the yard. Nancy was watching the hunt from the back door, and she hastily ran and shut the dogs out. By the time the huntsmen came up, the stag had mounted the manure heap and found its way out on the roof of Orr's pigsties.

'Them slates will never hold him,' shrieked Nancy. 'The Divil mend ye and your hunt.' As she spoke the forefeet of the stag went through the roof. A second later his hind legs disappeared; and there was the unfortunate animal wedged securely on the roof. As Nancy put it. 'He didn't know whether he was going or coming.'

'We must saw him out,' someone suggested.

'Aye, and let him fall in on my wee pigs,' expostulated Nancy.

'Never mind, woman,' said one of the officials, 'you'll be paid for the damage. That roof was done anyway. It's lucky the stag went through it before the next big wind.'

Nancy tossed her head and walked away. Certainly Frank had said something about the sties needing new roofs. She decided not to be drawn into any argument on the matter. The County Down Stag Hounds could well afford to pay for the damage they did, and anyway the roof would have done bravely for a lock of weeks yet.

The stag was sawn out and fell among the young pigs without doing any great damage to them or himself. A smiling, prosperous-looking man appeared on the scene and laid Nancy's economic fears at rest by assuring her that the damage would be paid. She departed cheerfully. Things might have been worse.

But the day's bad luck was not over.

The delay at the farm had enabled Marie and Tessie to catch up with the rest. Seeing that something unusual was taking place at the farm, curiosity increased Marie's nerve. She attempted to jump the hedge bordering the lane. Marie's idea of jumping was to get as close as possible to the obstacle, close her eyes tightly, and leave the rest to the horse. Her horse did its best, but was hardly expecting to land in a narrow lane; actually it landed in the far hedge. The betrayed animal uttered a frenzied, tearing scream, as grotesquely human as its wildly rearing, erect posture. Then it came down heavily. It gave a convulsive movement, like a deep shudder and lay still. It had broken its neck.

The crowd in the yard watched in horror. As Charles, white-faced, rushed towards his sister, he was prepared for the worst. A number of men followed him. Keen horse lovers though they were, they were, for the time being, indifferent to the fate of the noble animal, whose only mistake had been a too implicit obedience. All eyes were turned on the motionless figure of the girl.

'Is she dead?' asked someone, voicing the question in every mind.

Charles shook his head. 'No. Lend a hand there. Her leg is caught. That will do. Get something to carry her – a door – anything will do.'

They carried her into Orr's. The Hunt dispersed dispondently. Charles went for the doctor. Isobel and Nancy watched beside the unconscious girl. Nancy looked at the small, white face pityingly. In her riding kit, with her short black hair tumbling untidily about her ears, Marie looked a mere child. Nancy's heart went out to her with fierce, protective insistency. John Harkness's daughter, maybe, but just a little wee scrap of a hurt child. So this was the girl Peter had in his eye. The merciful Lord had likely broken her neck to save her heart.

Marie opened her eyes and smiled at Nancy. 'I fell off the horse,' she explained. 'I hurt my head. Peter said I wasn't to tell daddy.'

Nancy glanced questionly at Isobel. 'Should we give her brandy?'

'Perhaps a little,' said Isobel. 'She's got concussion.'

'I fell off the horse and hurt my head,' repeated Marie.

'Yes, I know,' said Isobel, soothingly. 'Lie still, you'll feel better in a minute.'

'I fell off the horse,' Marie insisted. 'Does Peter know that I fell off the horse?' She took the brandy quietly enough, but immediately began rambling again. 'Peter's going to be manager of the mill. But I mustn't tell daddy. Does daddy know I fell off the horse?'

Isobel drew Nancy aside. 'It may not be very serious, but she'll probably go on talking wildly all night. Do you think you could possibly keep her here?'

'If they let me,' whispered Nancy. 'I'll be only too pleased. But we'll have to be waiting to see what her brother says.'

The doctor arrived a few minutes later with Charles.

'She's come round,' said Isobel. 'But she's talking the wildest nonsense.'

The doctor glanced at her. 'She's not too bad. This the leg that was caught?' He turned accusingly to Charles. 'What was all the fuss about? She hasn't even broken her leg,' he said, as if this fact afforded him some disappointment. 'She's been lucky ... if she came down as you said.' He produced the inevitable tablets.

Isobel took the opportunity to hold a whispered consultation with Charles.

'She has slight concussion,' continued the doctor. 'You can move her safely enough, but get her to bed at once. She will probably talk incessantly for a bit, but that's nothing to worry about. Giver her two of these tablets and keep her as quiet as possible. If she does not sleep give her two every two hours until she drops off. Once she gets over she will probably sleep right through the next day, the longer the better. I shall call in sometime tomorrow forenoon.'

Charles looked enquiringly at Nancy. 'We do not want to give you any trouble, Mrs Orr.'

'I should like for her to stay,' said Nancy. 'Maybe it would be better to leave her here, doctor? It's quiet-like, and she maybe would get straight to sleep.'

The doctor was in a hurry. 'Yes, the less she's disturbed the better. Don't forget about the tablets, Mrs Orr. Somebody must stay with her tonight.'

'That will be all right, doctor,' said Nancy.

The doctor hurried off. Isobel and Nancy managed to get Marie to bed. She talked steadily right through the performance, back and forth over the same half-dozen sentences – the horse, Peter and her daddy occupying the main theme.

Nancy and Isobel left her for a few minutes in the hope that the absence of an audience might stem her discourse.

They joined Charles who was hanging about the hall looking as useless as he felt. 'I don't like giving you all this trouble,' he repeated to Nancy. 'I don't know what we ought to do.'

'If John Harkness hears the talk of her the Dear knows what will be the end of it,' said Nancy bluntly.

Isobel backed her up. 'Yes, Charles, it's far wiser to leave her here. She will probably be quite sensible in the morning.'

'But dad will be over like one bird when he hears,' Charles pointed out.

Nancy placed her hands on her hips and looked aggressive. 'You leave him to me,' she said. 'Yon lassie will be sleeping whenever I say she is. Anyone who talks of disturbing her will have me to reckon with.'

'Do you think you can manage my father?' asked Charles with a smile.

'Aye, and your grandfather if needs be. You two can be getting along as soon as you like. The girl will be all the better to be quit of ye for a bit.'

Having got rid of her visitors, Nancy gave Eliza a long list of complicated instructions and returned to her patient. Marie had just remembered that she had to buy face cream in Ballynahinch. Nancy discouraged the plan by casting libellous aspersions on all brands of face cream procurable in Ballynahinch, and persuaded Marie to content herself with two of the doctor's tablets. The patient gave way, but her recitation concerning the horse, Peter and daddy now contained frequent references to face cream. At long last Marie talked herself to sleep.

'Thank God for that!' Nancy reflected. 'If I'd listened to her any longer I'd have concussion myself.'

CHAPTER EIGHT

John Harkness arrived soon after Marie had fallen asleep. The importance of not disturbing anyone suffering from concussion had been duly instilled into him by Charles, and he gave Nancy little opportunity of testing her skill in managing him. He thanked her gravely for her kindness, offered to send out a nurse, which offer Nancy instantly rejected, and departed. Nancy was a little disappointed. She had prepared an effective speech for his special benefit, and, being an economical individual, she disliked the idea of good material going to waste. Of course, she told Frank what she would have said, but that was not quite so satisfactory. Nancy preferred the imperative to the conditional mood.

Later in the evening Peter arrived on the scene, so portions of the speech came in handy enough after all. Peter was worried. 'I heard she was talking nonsense,' he said. 'Has Mr Harkness been with her?'

Nancy sniffed more audibly than elegantly. 'She's been talking all right, and maybe it wasn't all nonsense. And anyway, what has Marie Harkness to do with you, Peter Montgomery?'

'Oh, nothing,' said Peter. 'I happened to be passing and I

thought I'd enquire about her.'

'And isn't it yourself that has the kind heart!' jeered his sister. 'It no stands to reason that anyone could go on thinking of themselves as much as you do, without tiring. It's right glad I am to see signs of a change. Have you been to enquire after your mother in her grand new house in Meadow Street yet?'

'No,' said Peter gruffly. 'Not yet.'

'Well, well! We musn't expect miracles all over the place,' remarked Nancy. 'I heard you had bought yon house and the one beside it forby. Taking up house property now, Peter?'

Peter glanced at her covertly. 'Yes, it's quite a paying proposition.'

'Is it now?' asked Nancy innocently. 'You seem to have struck a lock of paying propositions. But whose doing the paying?'

'Oh, I got the bank to advance me a loan,' explained Peter grandly. 'It was easy enough.'

'Some folks are quare and saft,' said Nancy. 'Here's me and Frank was thinking of raising a bit of money till buy some land as was going cheap, and didn't we think we could no raise it without mortgaging the farm? I never heard tell of it being so easy to get money out of a bank before.'

'Buying houses is different. You can always raise money for house property', Peter explained carefully.

'Oh, I see. You're sort of buying them on the instalment system, and paying interest on the money you've borrowed! Likely, it will turn out bravely for you, Peter. You were never one to draw the short straw.'

'I am usually fairly lucky,' Peter admitted. 'By the way, Nancy, I'd like to see Marie for a few minutes.'

'Marie?' questioned Nancy. 'Oh, you mean Miss Harkness?' She turned on him suddenly and fiercely. 'See here, Peter Montgomery, I know you so well I'd give you a knife this minute if I thought you'd cut your throat ... But you was born to be hanged, and it's no my place to be flying in the face of Providence. But you keep away from Marie Harkness. I'm warning you, and I'll no warn you twice.'

'I am not in the least interested in her,' said Peter quickly. 'I've tried to discourage her. She runs after me.'

Nancy clenched her fists. Her eyes were blazing. 'Merciful God, what did I ever do to have the likes of you for a brother! You was always above your own class, Peter. But there's no many of the village lads would say a thing like that about a lass, an' it were true even. But it's a lie, Peter, and well you know it. Get out of my house before I brain you, and so be you set foot on our land again I'll put the dogs on you. Get out!'

Peter rose sullenly. 'You've suddenly taken a great fancy to John Harkness's daughter,' he taunted.

'Maybe it's a family failing,' said Nancy.

'Well, I can tell you one thing,' replied Peter. 'If you mention Marie's ravings you'll get her into trouble as well as me.'

'It would be worth it,' snapped his sister. 'A wee sickness is better than a big funeral. Mind, I'll be watching you, Peter Montgomery, and I've good eyes till me' and she banged the door in his face. 'It's a pity the rat poison is so dear,' she informed the cat viciously.

After a night's sleep Marie was comparatively normal. She awoke about dinner time, and immediately enquired if she had fallen off the horse.

Nancy heaved a sigh. 'You've been falling off that horse since yesterday.'

'Have I?' said Marie with a smile. 'I can't remember anything about it. Where am I?'

Nancy explained as much as she thought necessary.

Marie became interested. 'You were Nancy Montgomery?

Weren't you? Then you're Peter Montgomery's sister?'

Nancy admitted the relationship with no great enthusiasm.

Marie looked at her shyly. 'Did I talk very much last night?'

'You did so,' said Nancy. 'Very wild kind of talk.'

'About Peter?'

Nancy nodded. 'Far too much about Peter. You're the very silly girl, Marie Harkness.'

Marie said nothing for some minutes. Then, 'I'm sorry I talked,' she said. 'We have not told anyone yet, not even my father.'

'Aye, I gathered that,' said Nancy. 'It's a great wonder you haven't more sense. Peter's in love with you I suppose?'

Marie nodded. 'And I'm in love with him. We are going to be married when daddy makes him manager of the mill.'

Nancy shook her head half-laughing. 'Girl, dear, have sense. Drink up your milk now like a good child or we'll be having the doctor and the whole family in on top of us before I've washed your face.'

Nancy was graver than usual as she bustled about her work. Marie Harkness was none of her business, and, if she had not the wit to see through Peter it was her own look out. But the vision of a small, crumpled figure persisted in intruding upon her matter-of-fact outlook. Surely Peter would have the sense to heed her warning; at heart he was an arrant coward. He'd never dare face the wrath of John Harkness. Nancy sighed heavily. Had Peter been a man of Frank's calibre how she would have gloried in the old man's discomfiture! But there it was. When she had wished John Harkness ill she had not wished him just as ill as this.

A week after Marie's accident Charles tendered his resignation at Ringawoody. John Harkness listened in silence. Charles explained briefly that he was getting married in the spring. In the meantime he had been given the opportunity of managing a spinning mill in the city. He mentioned another of Ringawoody's rivals, and, as the chance might not arise again, he had decided to accept the offer.

'And regarding your position as a director?' his father enquired.

Charles, himself, was too distressed at the prospect of leaving Ringawoody to realise that his father was trying to offer himself an excuse to modify his ultimatum. 'That is only a matter of form,' said Charles bluntly. 'There's never been more than one director in this firm. That was you, dad.'

'I was referring to the question of capital,' said John Harkness.

Charles shrugged. 'I suppose that roughly I have about €10,000 in the firm, though I doubt if it's worth half that. I'm not looking for a partnership anywhere in the meantime, and Ringawoody is as good an investment as anywhere else. Unless, of course, you object to my being a shareholder as well as an imaginary director.'

The two men looked at each other uneasily. John Harkness knew that his son was sparing Ringawoody. Pride might prevent the son from sparing the father, and the father from sparing the son, but pride must not threaten the foundations of Ringawoody. Both silently admitted that. Another heavy mortgage would practically place the mill in the hands of the bank.

'If that is your wish,' said John Harkness. 'I am quite agreeable. I am sorry you are leaving us. I suppose nothing I can say would infuence you to reconsider your decision?'

'Regarding my marriage with Isobel? No, father, I'm sorry, but that is definitely settled.'

'I wish you every happiness,' said John Harkness heavily. 'I suppose you want to get away at an early date?'

'Yes,' Charles agreed. 'I should like to get away as soon as you can find a new manager.'

'Very good,' said his father. 'I shall tell Montgomery to take over in the morning.'

Charles hesitated. 'I should get in a new man if I were you.'

'I have frequently told you, Charles, that I am quite capable of asking for your advice should I require it,' said John Harkness, ringing the bell for his secretary.

Peter Montgomery heard of his promotion with his usual agreeably servile smile.

'You have treated me very well, Mr Harkness,' he said with every appearance of earnestness; youthful sincere earnestness, 'and I shall endeavour to justify your confidence in me.'

John Harkness waved him away. 'I hope so, Montgomery, I hope so,' he muttered mechanically. He was too sick at heart to fnd comfort in the meaningless platitudes to which he normally paid appropriate courtesy. Edward – and now Charles! He had imagined at the time that the blow of Edward's desertion was the big disappointment of his life. But he had not greatly missed his elder son. True, he had received a bad shock. The fact that his policy should be questioned and rejected by a member of his own family distressed and grieved him, but, apart from the financial difficulty Edward's defection had affected him only in a sentimental manner. The loss of Charles seemed more fundamental. Charles's statement that there had been only one director in the firm was not perfectly correct. Charles had always argued about things. He had insisted on interfering. His father might reject his advice when it was thrust on him, but he frequently reconsidered it at a later date. As he considered the past John Harkness realised, with reluctance, that during the previous ten years most of the more successful alterations that had been undertaken by the firm had been originated by Charles. He had realised that Edward had had a grievance, and he had forced himself to relinquish to his younger son much of the control he had so jealously guarded. Charles should not have the same complaint. But his sacrifice had availed nothing. A hysterical chit of a mill girl meant more to Charles than his father's pride or the dignity of Ringawoody. Almost pathetically he had, as it were, offered his most treasured possession as a bribe to keep his son by his side, and he had rejected it. John Harkness looked an old man, and he felt an old man. Even his pride afforded him very little comfort.

Perhaps at the moment there hovered near him that dangerous form of lunacy, in which one wonders for one distressing but mercifully brief moment of lucidity if one's gilt-edged securities are either gilt-edged or secure.

Bright Point-to-Point Races were held early in March that year. The Meeting was popular, attracting big crowds, and arousing much interest even among a community regarding gambling, in any shape or form, as an uneconomic proposition – if not a serious vice. Evangelical ministers have been known to back horses in the Derby because the Derby is 'different.' Canny, pious, half-Scottish, wholly Ulster farmers back horses at Bright Races because Bright Races are an institution. Ulster has a genuine respect for institutions. Most of the respectable, restrainedly good-humoured crowd who patronise Bright, March after March, know the history of every horse on the card, from its birth onward. Fortunes are never made or lost. The odds are never attractive. The 'Ten to one bar four' legend of the bookies simply means that the four horses which will take part in the race start at something like three to five; while the half-dozen entrants that have been withdrawn, could have been backed at ten to one, had anyone been so misinformed as to back them; but since they are not running the danger does not arise. There are, occasionally, surprises even at Bright, and when a surprise crops up it is a big one, because no true County Down man could be persuaded, before the race, that an outsider stands a chance against the home stock. To have been born and bred in the county, and, furthermore, never to have been out of the county, is about the highest testimonial a Downshire man would ask of man or beast.

On the morning of the Races, Isobel Martin arrived with her uncle and aunt and two sisters in the trap. It was a wet day, but there was a large gathering in the field. Already the crowds were melting away from the bookies and moving towards the hill which overlooked the course in anticipation of the first race.

'There's Charles over there,' said Bridgit. 'Go and ask him what's going to win.'

Isobel studied a board in front of her, and Charles and Edward strolled up to offer advice.

'Any of those first three might pull it off,' said Edward. 'It's a sheer chance which one.'

Charles, Edward and David Martin were each prepared to back a different horse, but all were agreed that the winner was in the first three mentioned on the board. Isobel continued to examine the list.

'Tessie, you back uncle's choice. Bridgit will back Edward's. Charles can back his own. I'm going to back Stephanie at fourteen to one.'

The men were genuinely shocked. 'But we've never heard of Stephanie!' they gasped.

'I don't believe there is such a horse,' said Charles.

'It's likely some old, done-out beast with the name changed,' insisted David Martin.

'I am going to back Stephanie,' said Isobel. 'Uncle, can you lend me half-a-crown?'

'Not to back Stephanie. I'll put five shillings on Johnny for you if you like.'

'I don't like,' said Isobel. 'Charles, lend me half-a-crown.'

'No,' said Charles flatly. 'I will not.'

'Did anyone ever meet such a set of obliging men?' said Isobel, half annoyed. She turned to Edward, as she believed. 'Surely you will not refuse to lend a respectable woman a paltry half-crown?' she held out a hand in affected despair.

The others turned away in evident amusement, and Isobel glanced up swiftly to perceive that she had been addressing John Harkness, who had just arrived on the scene with Marie. She drew a sudden breath. 'It's very wet, isn't it?' she ejaculated uneasily.

John Harkness smiled. She reminded him a little of Marie in one of her more childlike moments of confusion. 'Very wet,' he agreed. 'These young men have no consideration, keeping you begging for half-crowns in this downpour.' He gave her the coin.

Isobel was miserably embarrassed. 'Uncle, you owe Mr Harkness for this,' she said, looking reproachfully at her uncle.

'Indeed I do not,' said her uncle. 'You can pay him out of your winnings, and I fancy he's going to be unlucky. Perhaps you didn't know that she's going to back Stephanie, Mr Harkness?'

Isobel strode off indignantly, and John Harkness and David Martin moved together leisurely towards the hill.

'How is farming?' enquired John Harkness conversationally.

'Improving slightly. I think we've turned the corner now. About time, too.'

John Harkness nodded. 'Yes, times were bad. I was sorry about Hugh. He went down badly.'

'He did.'

'The three children are with you in Dromara?'

'Yes, they are now.'

John Harkness glanced at him curiously. 'Is the young

lady a relation of your wife?'

'Isobel?' asked David Martin. 'No, she's Hugh's eldest girl.' He looked at the millowner straightly. 'I was sorry to know there was trouble between you and Charles about her. You know your own business best, Mr Harkness, but Isobel Martin has refused as good as your son ... and better. He could have gone further and fared very much worse.'

John Harkness said nothing. The two men had reached the crest of the hill and stood waiting for the horses to line up. 'I like the look of Isobel's Stephanie,' said John Harkness.

'H'mm,' grunted David Martin. 'I'll watch her run before I pass an opinion.' He lit his pipe and turned again to the older man. A slow suspicion was gradually gaining weight in his mind. He had not forgotten the mystery of the anonymous purchaser of the Dromara farm. 'I am a plain man, Mr Harkness,' he said slowly, 'and I spoke plainly. I may say that I took it ill that you would consider Hugh's daughter beneath your son – very ill indeed.' He gave John Harkness another long, straight look. 'I had every reason to think from a certain action of yours that you wished Hugh's children well.'

John Harkness said nothing.

David Martin held out his hand. 'I'm not thanking you, John Harkness. As far as I am concerned I'd rather labour on the road than accept a penny from any man alive, and I fancy that you are about the last man to whom Isobel would wish to be under an obligation. But as things have turned out, the two younger girls will benefit most, and for their sakes I am very grateful. But I consider that you hold a mortgage on the farm. Sooner or later it will be paid.'

'I was under many an obligation to Hugh,' said John Harkness.

'That's as may be,' said David Martin. 'But Hugh's children will be reared on charity no longer than I can help.

We must make the rig build the dike – even if it's a high one. I'll be looking round for my family. I wish you good day, John Harkness,' and the farmer turned away.

John Harkness stood watching the field. Marie and Margaret, accompanied by the three little boys, joined him. Marie complained crossly of the weather. She was annoyed with Peter. She knew that he had arrived, as she had seen him in the distance with Mr Henderson, the newly-appointed secretary, but he was deliberately avoiding her because her father was there. When Marie compared his behaviour with that of Charles and Isobel she became increasingly indignant. As the race started, Edward came up. Charles and Isobel had been with him, but they stood a little way back from the others. Isobel would not be drawn into the family group while John Harkness was present.

'They're off!'

There was a moment's silence followed by an excited buzz of chatter as the horses took the first ditch. The ground was soft and treacherous, but all the horses cleared the jump without mishap. The three favourites were to the front with Johnny leading by half a head. The rest of the field straggled. Stephanie was close behind the first three running easily and smoothly. There was a high hedge at the bottom of the first field. Johnny took it badly and lost his lead to the second favourite. The third favourite bungled it and came down.

'That's Edward's choice out of it,' said Isobel.

Charles nodded. 'Yes, and I'm afraid Johnny is off his form too. I'd lend you that half-crown now, Isobel, 'this, as Stephanie's performance at the hedge raised an astonished cheer from the crowd.

'You can keep it,' Isobel told him.

The horses disappeared from view and the crowd waited impatiently concentrating on the far hill where the field would reappear for the homeward race. The placing at that point was considered important. A few minutes passed.

'Here they are!'

Glasses were raised.

'Johnny leads!' – 'That strange, wee mare is going well!' – 'It's anyone's race yet!'

The crowd groaned as Chance, the second favourite was passed by Stephanie who was now moving like a thoroughly roused volcano.

'Come on, Johnny!' roared the crowd, forgetting its respectability for the moment, in its excitement. Johnny came on; a sound, steady goer was Johnny. Johnny was used to winning races, but he wasn't going to win this one if Stephanie knew anything about it.

'He's beat!' said an old farmer, in about the same tone as he would have said, 'The Nationalist has got in.'

And beaten he was. Stephanie came down the hill, an excited streak of lightning. Neck and neck the two horses cleared the stream. For a second it looked as if Johnny might still argue the point, but only for a second. This kind of thing was outside Johnny' experience, and he was much too Northern to attempt the impossible. Stephanie shot ahead without an effort. One of the biggest shocks Bright had experienced in years.

To say that Isobel was jubilant is to stop at the beginning of the story. 'How much is fourteen half-crowns – no, fifteen half-crowns, Charles?' she asked with innocent maliciousness.

Charles smiled. 'Now, you can give dad back his half-crown. See you thank him nicely.'

Isobel flushed; where John Harness was concerned she has absolutely no sense of humour. She knew that Charles was laughing at her, but, nevertheless, she determinedly repaid her future father-in-law. To add to the embarrassment of the proceeding, when she had reclaimed her winnings she found herself the centre of quite a gathering.

'Where did you get that tip?'

'You are a close one and no mistake!'

'Some folks don't believe in giving their friends a chance!' Her uncle professed to be particularly grieved. 'I'm surprised at you, Isobel, keeping a good thing like that up your sleeve.'

Isobel wished that she did not feel so ridiculously nervous. She glanced at John Harkness. 'Mr Harkness, here's your half-crown.' She vainly hoped that her voice sounded casual.

John Harkness accepted the coin. He would have spared her had it been in his power to do so. He saw, that for some inexplicable reason, she was intensely distressed and nervous. He had no desire to add to her agitation. In fact he was inclined to be sorry that her attitude towards himself was so obviously hostile.

Charles, however, refused to let her off so easily. 'Listen to her! Dad, if I were you, I should insist on claiming half her winnings. You put up the cash and you ran all the risk. It's downright fraud.' He unclasped Isobel's clenched fingers and displayed her wealth with loud amazement. 'Just look at what she's trying to stick to. We can't encourage daylight robbery.

John Harkness looked frowningly at the girl's trembling lips. 'Don't be silly, Charles,' he said sharply.

Charles glanced at Isobel, and too late, realised his stupidity. He tried to draw her away without avail.

Isobel dropped her winnings on the ground with a gesture of distaste. 'It was your half-crown won,' she said childishly to John Harkness. 'I don't want any of it.'

Marie, sensing an atmosphere she could not understand, broke in quickly. 'Isobel, that's unkind to daddy. You shouldn't blame him for Charles's silly joke.'

Isobel moved away. She had made a fool of herself, probably amused John Harkness, and most certainly she had not improved matters for Charles. She wished damply that she was dead and buried.

The rest of the company looked uncomfortable, but David Martin laughed the matter off. 'She's been touchy ever since she had the 'flu. She'll come round.'

In the meantime, the three youngest Harknesses were busily engaged in recovering Isobel's abandoned treasure, a proceeding which Bridgit was disputing with some wrath. The youngsters quite evidently had no mistaken views about the value of perfectly good half-crowns.

Charles departed to make his peace with Isobel and found her sitting dejectedly in the back of his car. He knew that the slightest sign of sympathy would reduce her to tears. He offered none. 'I don't think there was any necessity for you to be so rude to dad,' he said quietly.

'I knew you were angry,' said the girl wearily. 'I wish I'd stayed at home. I always make a fool of myself when your father is about. I should have known.'

Charles gave her a cigarette, and shook her affectionately. 'You're a bad girl. You could get on with my father if you wanted to,' he said more regretfully than he quite intended.

Isobel studied the grey, sodden landscape with an expression as cheerful as the weather. 'I do want to. I know you are terribly cut about all this – leaving Ringawoody and everything. I thought that you and your father did not get on very well, and that it might be as well if you did leave. But, now, I see that I was mistaken. He's dreadfully fond of you, Charles ... I think that's why I am so nervous of him. He likes you far more than Edward.'

Charles moved uncomfortably. 'I wouldn't say that,' he said uneasily. 'But, naturally, dad was disappointed when Edward left. He makes an unholy fuss about little things, but when anything really matters to him he says very little. Apart from anything, I hate leaving Ringawoody. I wish I knew just what my father thought. It's quite possible that he is relieved. I know he likes things run in his own way. He liked us to be there if we didn't interfere too much. I've been taking things out of his hands lately. I think that he allowed me to do so because he knew that it would not be for long. I may be wrong, of course. I wish I knew definitely.'

'You are wrong,' said Isobel decidedly. 'He doesn't want you to go. I think you ought to stay, Charles.'

Charles did not reject the idea with the scorn many a less sincere man might have assumed. 'Perhaps I ought,' he said slowly. 'But I don't think that sacrifices of that nature are often successful. It wouldn't be fair to you or me. If he had any real reason for his attitude it would be different. But as things stand, if I gave you up I should feel resentful, and doing it like that is not going to help anyone. There would be far more ill-will between us, if I accepted his conditions and stayed than there could be if we carry out our original plan.'

It was, perhaps, not the kind of speech that would have produced a demonstration of affection from every girl. But Isobel and Charles understood each other better than most young couples. They would both have been much happier if they could have exercised the same understanding on a wider circle. But, as Charles said, it is an age of specialisation.

CHAPTER NINE

Spring came to Ringawoody with its familiar, ever novel variety. The monotony of spring in the country is like the monotony of a Christmas stocking; a kind of joyful certainty of surprises, repeated year after year, but always excitingly different.

First snowdrops, first primroses, first lambs turn up every year, but they are never twice the same. Nature, like an astute pantomine producer, takes infinite pains to vary the programme. Perhaps the snow drops are put back a little in the opening procession to give the celandines more limelight. Sometimes the primroses are cut down to half their usual numbers to divert attention to the wild cherry blossom. Last year the daffodils tried to push themselves forward. Daffodils are inclined to blow their own beautiful, golden trumpets. This year they are more subdued, making every effort to carry out instructions and restrain their innate desire of applause.

The lambs have learned brand new tricks, though they are as much to the forefront as ever. Lambs have made a name for themselves, as appealingly timid little creatures. They take advantage of their lamb-like reputations to behave in a manner quite out of keeping with the name.

Farmers' wives know this well. But the sad, destitute little creature, who has perhaps lost its mother, looks very different from the unmanageable little rascal that made such a nuisance of itself last year. No one has the heart to leave it to its fate. The poor, wee thing becomes a pet. It also becomes a perfect pest.

This year the Orrs had only one pet lamb. The year before they had had three, and Nancy had dared Frank to say pet lamb to her again. But even Nancy was no match for the wiles of Rosie. Rosie was born delicate, and her mother refused to own her. After examining Rosie dispassionately, one was forced to the conclusion that she had some reason for her distaste. Rosie's neck was a peculiar shape, her head was very much to one side, and one of her legs was shorter than the other three.

In order to save her authority Nancy pretended to agree with Frank's diffident assurance that the lamb would not live for more than a day or two. The inevitable feeding bottles were brought down from the attic, and the troublesome routine commenced – and continued. Rosie threw off her delicacy – in every sense of the word – and lived to be a greater trial than the three previous warriors put together.

Pet lambs are usually claimed as the personal property of the children in a farmhouse. They prepare the feeding bottles and encourage their charges on the paths of villainy. In a short time the pet lamb becomes startlingly like a naughty child – pert, wilful, and noisy. At best, pet lambs tend to become troublesome, but the Orrs' Rosie was in a class by herself. The twist in her neck may have warped her nature, but certainly Rosie had more un-sheep like qualities than is customary even in a pet lamb.

Before she passed all bounds she had a champion in Marie Harkness. Since her accident, Marie had developed a liking for Nancy, and had formed the habit of coming over to Ballycam frequently. She was greatly taken by Rosie's endearing tricks, and accused Nancy of stony-hearted cruelty when she would have put her foot down at an early stage and banished Rosie from the house. The poor little thing was cold. The poor little thing was also lonely and unhappy, you could tell by the way it cried. Out of politeness to an important visitor the poor little thing was allowed to become an imposition beside which Land Annuities pale into insignificance.

Marie was very happy that spring. Since the Bright Races, Peter had apparently overcome his fear of her father. While he still advised caution, he was more confident. With the removal of Edward and Charles from the firm he knew himself to be fairly free from antagonistic supervision. He had never had any difficulty in persuading the Head of the Firm that he was a worthy young man. He was perfectly aware that the mill, as a whole, resented his promotion, but Peter throve on the resentment of those whom he considered beneath his notice. His mother and younger sisters were no longer in evidence; though he was intensely conscious of the disadvantages of possessing a family whose social inferiority was, in Peter's opinion, all too apparent. He hoped his skeletons in the cupboard might be more or less forgotten. He was coming round to the view, that Marie, far from marrying beneath her, was very fortunate in gaining the serious attentions of so progressive a young man as himself. Had it not been for his old, habitual awe of John Harkness he would have been positively bumptious. As it was, he was pleasantly sure of himself, and he assured Marie that when Charles was married he would ask her father's consent to become officially engaged to her. In the meantime, it was perhaps just as well to be discreet. He saw her frequently but not too obviously, and gave her expensive presents, for which her father paid, without being aware of his own generosity.

Rosie, the lamb, was the means of casting the first

shadow on Marie's peace of mind. When Marie began her visits to Ballycam she was unaware of the far from cordial relations existing between Nancy and her brother, and she hoped to be able to discuss her romance with her new friend. She soon learned her mistake. Peter seized the first opportunity to warn her against mentioning his name to Nancy, and Nancy herself obviously wanted to hear nothing about him. Marie, therefore, kept her own counsel, leaving Nancy with the impression that Peter had heeded her warning.

One morning Nancy left on the early bus to visit her mother. Mrs, Montgomery had been in poor health since she went to the city, and Nancy was worried about her. She arranged to return on the half-three bus. Marie had asked her to bring her home some wool, and since she was dining out with her father the same evening, she was to come along at four o'clock in order to collect her property and allow her time to be at 'Craigaveagh' by seven.

The afternoon was one of those deceptively sunny affairs that convince the most cautious that rain is a myth. Though it was a longish walk to Ballycam, Marie decided that it would be a shame to waste the sunshine. She set out in high spirits, and what with stopping to gather primroses and investigate birds' nests it was after three before she arrived in Ballynahinch. To make up for lost time she decided to take the short cut through the fields; even the marsh could not be too marshy on such a marvellous day. The marsh, however, proved very squelchy. The weather, considering it had done very well for one day, forgot its earlier promise, and produced an unnecessarily refreshing shower of rain. Marie was wet before she reached Ballycam, especially about the feet.

Eliza was waiting impatiently for Nancy's arrival. 'The bus is maybe late,' she said gloomily. 'And it's me half-day. I was going to see me aunt in Crossgar.'

Marie removed her stockings and hung them over a chair

to dry before the range. 'Find me a pair of Mrs Orr's slippers and then you can go. I'll wait and explain to Mrs Orr,' she said good-naturedly.

Eliza cheered up. 'Wouldn't you be wanting stockings, Miss? And will I no make you a cup of tea before I go?' she asked.

Marie shook her head. 'No thanks, Eliza, my own won't be many minutes drying, and I can have a cup of tea with Mrs Orr when she comes in.'

When Eliza had set off, Marie settled herself to dry. The kitchen was warm, her chair was comfortable, and Marie was a little tired after her walk. She dropped over into a light doze.

On this pretty picture of domestic peace intruded Rosie. Rosie was even less amiably disposed than usual. She had been driven from what she considered her natural habitat, with more vigour than politeness, by an irritated Eliza, who found some temporary compensation for her vanishing half-day in contemplating the hinterland of Rosie vanishing from her newly-scrubbed kitchen. Rosie was not prepared to enter into argument with a common farm servant, especially as that servant was possessed of a particularly lusty arm. She retired to the barn and brooded over the unfair conditions that handicap semi-orphaned lambs in the fight for comfort. Her reflections had much the same effect on her as a contemplation of the historic spider had on Robert the Bruce. There was nothing like having another go at it. She returned to the door and pushed, then she paused. The door made no resistance but Rosie knew from experience that the door was the least of her obstacles. As no outcry greeted her first manœuvre, she ventured into the scullery. Still no signs of an attack from the enemy. Rosie became arrogant, she walked boldly into the kitchen. Nothing happened. Rosie pattered round to satisfy herself that nothing had been seriously disturbed during her absence. She then displaced the cat and disposed herself contentedly over the fender. If Rosie had stopped at this she might have retained Marie's warm heart to the day she was translated into chops. But stopping anywhere was not one of Rosie's most marked characteristics. The real essence of comfort was marred for Rosie by the absence of those who challenged her rights to such comfort. Rosie became bored and looked round for some convenient amusement. Marie's stockings were within easy reach. Rosie dragged them off the chair and investigated them. The investigation did not improve Rosie's knowledge nor the shape of Marie's hose. It might be said in Rosie's defence that she was not aware that these peculiar articles were designed as footwear. She assumed that they were some unusual form of titbit, and she proceeded to eat them; not that she thought much of them as a delicacy, but it was something to do.

Marie awoke with a start and a crick in her neck. It was beginning to get dark. She looked at the clock; half-past five and no sign of Nancy. She must have missed the bus. It was just as well she had arranged for the men to have tea at Mrs O'Kelly's. Marie got up lazily, stretching herself comfortably. She would have to go now. She couldn't wait for Nancy or the wool. She remembered her stockings and awakened more completely. And then she became aware of Rosie and her true depths of wickedness ...

'My stockings!' she wailed. 'Oh, you wicked lamb!'

Rosie was prepared to abandon all further claim to the stockings or what was left of them, but human beings have no sense of gratitude. The tender-hearted young lady who had so often championed the cause of Rosie with soft, beguiling endearments now showed herself in her true colours. Tender-hearted! Rosie smiled about it bitterly afterwards; just now she had to concentrate on evading the wild virago who attacked her without provocation. Marie seized the first available weapon, which proved to be the kitchen poker; even the common servant had contented herself with the broom, the poker indicated a greater degree of unscrupulousness. Rosie deftly evaded the first onslaught and retired under the table, from which retreat she hopefully tried the effect of her most melancholy 'Ba!' Her effort was wasted. Marie was deaf to melancholy 'Ba's.' She landed a neat wallop on the most accessible part of Rosie's anatomy, and followed it up with a vicious kick. This, Rosie considered, was a bit too much of a good thing. A fight was interesting, and nobody appreciated a rough house more than Rosie, but she had her standards of decency beyond which she would not go. She might be a lone, destitute lamb, unloved and unwanted, but she would not be kicked and smitten with pokers to please anyone.

She came out into the open and baaed indignantly. Marie ignored her passionate and eloquent protest. For all the effect her speech produced it might have been made in the House of Commons by any ordinary backbencher. Rosie's confidence was shattered. A few more skelps from Marie's poker completed the job. Rosie overthrew as many of the kitchen chairs as she could, that being her method of slamming the door and hastily withdrew. Her reign as a pet lamb was over. Marie told on her, the vindictive clipe, and she never got back.

Having banished Rosie and given vent to some of her fury, Marie paused to consider her predicament. If she caught the half-six bus from Ballynahinch she could still get home in time. But she could not go home on the bus without stockings. She ought to have accepted Eliza's offer earlier. It was perfectly sickening. She longed to murder Rosie slowly and very painfully. Ten minutes passed in indignant but useless recrimination.

Marie took another look at the clock. Nancy might not come until the nine bus. It was silly to sit doing nothing about it. There must be a pair of stockings somewhere in the house, and Nancy wouldn't mind. She found a small lamp and lit it. Thus armed she proceeded along the passage and upstairs to Nancy's room. Nancy was a methodical person, and Marie had no difficulty in finding stockings. She put them on and retraced her steps in a much more cheerful frame of mind. A draught on the stairs blew out the lamp. She gave a little exclamation of annoyance, for it was now almost quite dark and the passage from the hall to the kitchen was particularly obscure. She proceeded cautiously and suddenly paused with her hand on the knob of the kitchen door.

Two people had entered the kitchen and were talking angrily. They were Nancy and Peter. Marie hesitated. Peter did not like her visiting his sister, and if she showed herself he might easily say something that would hurt Nancy. In any case they seemed to be annoyed, and it might be as well to wait until Peter left. Even if she missed the bus now Nancy would lend her Frank's car. That she was overhearing a conversation not intended for her ears did not strike Marie at first, and when the fact was brought home to her she was much too interested in the conversation to be scrupulous about the matter.

Nancy was white and tired. She had found her mother dangerously ill, a condition for which she blamed Peter entirely. She was in no mood to be tactful. Not that Nancy was ever very much in that mood.

Peter, too, was not in an amiable humour. He had met Nancy by accident in Ballynahinch. She had requested, or rather ordered him to come up to the house with her, and he guessed that this was not so much a desire for his company as something unpleasant about his mother. Peter disliked unpleasant news, and at the moment he was too taken up by his many plans to have time for other people's troubles. He was inclined to admit that he had been a little premature in some of his financial arrangements, and any kind of investigation into the firm's accounts would be awkward. Peter believed that there was not the slightest danger of such an investigation for some considerable time:

but that kind of thing can be quite worrying. He had most assuredly plenty to think about without being bothered with outside fuss.

'Well?' he said roughly. 'What is it? I thought you did not want to see me here again?'

'If you'd go on thinking like that you'd keep fairly straight,' said Nancy. 'I don't want to see you, but your poor, misguided mother has no the same sense. She's asking for you.'

'I'm afraid I'm not interested,' said Peter sullenly. 'Mother knows perfectly well that I am busy.'

'I suppose you're no interested in the fact that she has pneumonia, that she's lying at death's door, that you brought her there by sending her off to where she was no used to living ... It's nothing to do with you, is it, Peter?'

'I know she is ill. Bessie wrote and told me so. But be reasonable, Nancy. What good can I do? Mother always imagines she's dying if she's the least bit sick. She will be all right in a few days. I can let her have a few pounds if she needs anything.'

'To the devil with you and your few pounds!' stormed Nancy. 'Have you no shred of decency in you at all, Peter Montgomery? I'd rather drown myself as ask you to do anything for me. But she's dying, Peter, and she's asking for you. You can no refuse, even you, Peter.'

Peter swore a particularly foul oath. It sounded strange from his lips, for Peter seldom swore. 'You're making the whole thing up. It's just a trick to drag me up there. I'm fed up with you, Nancy, and your damned interfering. Why can't you leave me alone?'

'I could have interfered plenty if so be I'd the motion, Peter, and well you know it,' said Nancy threateningly. 'You'd have come the queer flop if you had no dropped that carry-on with Marie Harkness. If you've a head on you at all you know that rightly. I'm thinking you thought better of it or you would no have heeded me, and I advise you to think better of ignoring your mother's dying wish.'

'I heeded you because I was not much taken with Marie Harkness, but I'm beginning to see I was a fool. I'd have got round her father easy enough. I'm not afraid of him, or of you either. You can keep your advice.'

Peter had been drinking, a habit he had formed only very recently. He had made the discovery that brandy gave him courage and helped him to dispel certain fears.

Nancy looked at him scornfully. 'You're drunk. That kind of courage no lasts long, Peter. But, drunk or sober, you'll go and see your mother this night. I'm telling you, Peter ... and I'll stop at nothing. I promised me mother you'd go, and go you will.'

Peter avoided her eyes. He was thoroughly exasperated and anxious to escape as soon as possible. 'Oh, all right. I'll go. But in future mind your own business and leave me to mind mine.' He strode from the room in anger.

Nancy sank into the armchair and sobbed from sheer exhaustion.

Marie came to her, a little wraith out of the darkness. 'Nancy, don't cry. It will be all right now. He's going to go. Oh, I was so frightened that he wouldn't.'

Nancy stared at her. 'You were there all the time!'

'Yes. I was up in your room for a pair of stockings. Rosie ate mine. When I came down you and Peter were here and I didn't like to come in.'

'Well, you see what he's like,' said Nancy. 'Maybe you realise you were well quit of him now?'

'He didn't know what he was saying,' said Marie unhappily. 'He was drunk. Peter would never speak like that if he were sober.'

'I'd rather have him drunk as sober any day,' said Nancy. 'Though that's saying mighty little. But never worry yourself, girl. It's time you were out of this.'

'Have I time for the bus?'

Nancy looked at the clock. 'I wouldn't say it. Frank is in the yard now, tell him to run you home.'

Marie went with a heavy heart. She put in a sleepless night. By morning she convinced herself that it was unfair to judge a man when he was drunk. Peter did not drink as a general rule, and that kind of thing would never happen again. Besides Nancy was unkind to him and brought out the worst in him. It was childish to expect that any man was absolutely perfect. Even Charles who came nearest Marie's conception of the ideal man, could say some exceedingly nasty things when he was out of temper. She found it hard to to forgive Peter's remark about herself, but doubtless he would explain that.

Peter explained it. He was tenderly contrite. He had never believed himself capable of such conduct. He was devoted to his mother and out of his mind with worry about her; it was just that Nancy rubbed him up the wrong way. They had never got on. Oh, yes, she was a good sort, but she had a grudge against him. He knew he had his failings, but Nancy was hard on him. If Marie turned against him now he would throw everything up. Life simply would not be worth living. He knew he deserved it. But Marie had always been tolerant and understanding, it would not be like her to throw a man over because he was foolish enough to take too much brandy once. He would never touch the stuff again. It altered a man's whole nature.

Nancy would have had an apt reply to the last statement, but Marie had none. She forgave Peter. However, she did not forgive the pet lamb. Rosie had deprived her of more than a pair of silk stockings. The first unfavourable view of the character of one's beloved is always a tragedy, though the character be a figment of the imagination and the love a romantic illusion.

CHAPTER TEN

Isobel Martin was like Charles Harkness in many ways. Now that she had the time, instead of devoting herself to dreaming of Charles and sewing trifles, she turned energetically to the task of assisting her uncle in the management of the farm.

At first, David Martin was dubious about her suggestions, but Isobel had perseverance as well as energy, and in time her uncle realised that many of her schemes, after suitable cropping and modification, might prove fairly successful. He liked her companionship on his rounds, and, when he accustomed himself to the idea, he approved of her interest in the work.

At the time of his conversation with John Harkness, David Martin had no intention of betraying his suspicion, which during that conversation had become a certainty regarding the identity of the mysterious philanthropist. David Martin was not a communicative man, and he had seen the trouble incurred by unnecessary talk. But as he watched Isobel's efforts to increase the value of the property, he was conscious of a growing sense of responsibility and uneasiness. She thought more of the ultimate good of the land than of securing high profits immediately. She was insistent in her demand that every available shilling should go back into the farm. She brought home books and catalogues, and talked of new machinery and expensive fertilisers. She proclaimed that Irish farming had been run on an unbusinesslike footing far too long. The farmers were too wrapped up in their bank balances, with the result that most of the balances had tipped over and developed into overdrafts. You could not expect to get money out of a business nowadays unless you put money into it. There was no economy in running the ship for a happorth of tar. And so on ...

There was wisdom in her remarks, but David Martin doubted if she would pursue the same policy if she knew the full facts of the case; and, after careful deliberation, he came to the conclusion that it was not fair to keep her in ignorance of an important consideration.

One evening, when uncle and niece were returning together from Downpatrick Market, where they had made an excellent sale of the lambs, Isobel remarked on the number of lambs they had lost that year owing to the bad weather. Mountainy lambs are easily lost. In the lambing season the ewes often wander far afield; without constant watching the mother gets into a predicament in the hills and the lambs frequently perish before she is discovered. The haphazard plan of leaving things to take their course and hoping for the best infuriated Isobel.

'Next year we are going to build a decent shelter and employ two extra men – good men – who know something about mountainy sheep. We lost nearly half the lambs this year through sheer neglect.'

Her uncle nodded. 'But we both put in a good deal of hard work,' he reminded her.

'Oh, I know. But I'm no use. I don't know the hills, and I know next to nothing about sheep. You have more than enough to do without the sheep. We can't expect the men to work miracles. They are overworked as it is. We'll have to get special help for the job next time.'

'We would need to increase the stock a good deal to make that pay,' said her uncle.

Isobel nodded. 'We will. I've a scheme to try a new breed here. Those ewes of ours are good stock in their way, but they breed too few lambs to make them a really paying proposition.'

Her uncle shook his head. 'You won't get a horned ewe to breed more than two or three lambs; one or two is a good average.'

'That's because you stick to the one strain and don't experiment. Farmers have a whole lot of silly maxims that haven't the slightest foundation to them, except their own dislike of anything that looks like a change,' replied Isobel forcefully. 'I quite see that you cannot expect the same numbers as from lowland stock, but the numbers could be increased. Anyway I'm going to invest in some new stock and give it a trial.'

'It's going to be an expensive experiment,' said her uncle.

Isobel began to make calculations. 'We can afford it. It's not as if we owed the bank anything. We are better off than most of the local farmers. Now that we are out of difficulties is the time to make improvements.'

'Aye,' smiled her uncle drily, 'and get into fresh ones. But as a matter of fact, Isobel, we are not out of difficulties. You and the two wee ladies don't own one acre of the farm yet.'

Isobel stared at him. 'Then you know who bought it for us?' she demanded.

'Yes,' said her uncle, 'and I don't think you'll be prepared to accept any gifts from him when you know. It was John Harkness.'

Isobel turned white. 'You are quite sure?' she asked slowly.

'Quite.'

'But I don't understand. Charles told me that he knew nothing about it.'

'Probably Charles knew nothing about it. It's not the kind of arrangement John Harkness would be proud of. I hardly think he would consider it necessary to mention it,' David Martin remarked.

'But why on earth should he do such a thing?' protested the girl, as though anxious to prove the impossibility of her uncle's suggestion. 'John Harkness lost thousands during the linen slump; he's not a rich man now. Charles thinks he mortgaged Ringawoody to buy Edward out, and yet you say that at that very time he turned round and bought this place for us. Why?'

David Martin shook his head. 'He's an odd man. Of course fifteen hundred pounds is not a big sum to a man who thinks in thousands, and he thought a good deal of your father.'

Isobel's lips tightened. 'But he doesn't think much of his daughter.'

Her uncle looked at her curiously. 'I think that is largely your own fault, Isobel. You must see the man's point of view as well as your own. He did not know, until very recently, that you were Hugh Martin's daughter. I thought all the more of you for trying to find a job when things went against us, but all men don't look at things in the same way. As far as John Harkness was concerned you were an ordinary mill girl. You cannot expect a mill owner to regard a marriage between his son and one of his most insignificant workers with much favour. Apart from the question of unsuitability that kind of thing is bad for the firm. Whatever may be said of farms, mills must be run on a businesslike basis. Maybe John Harkness carries things too far, but I see his point. It's a pity you ever went into the mill.'

Isobel shivered. 'I'm cold,' she explained. And a little later, added, 'John Harkness must be paid.'

Isobel worried at the problem until her head ached. If she had only known before the girls were brought home; but even then could she have let her pride drive her beloved Uncle David and her aunt from their old home? It wasn't fair to make things so hard to decide. John Harkness had no right to interfere. Had there been no option but to go they would have had to accept the inevitable. After all they were resigned to it. Her uncle had been promised a land steward's job near Downpatrick, and he might have been quite content. But even as she tried to believe this, Isobel knew that his heart was in his own farm. Anyway the option had been granted. Isobel, herself, had insisted on bringing Tessie and Bridgit home immediately. She had regarded the farm as hers, and now she must shoulder the responsibility and settle her account with John Harkness.

She had dreamed happily of making it such a grand place, better than the Knoll in its rosiest days, and bequeathing it to her uncle in trust for Tessie and Bridgit when she left to marry Charles. They had decided to wait until June for the wedding to give Isobel a chance to lend a hand at home. She smiled a little sadly as she remembered that many of her bright ideas had run far beyond June. Of course, her uncle could have carried out the sheep scheme; it would have been a splendid thing, but now out of the question. John Harkness must be paid.

She took a notebook and pencil and worked out innumerable mathematical possibilities which she knew only too well to be practical impossibilities. Even, with luck, it would take years to pay the debt. John Harkness must wait, and the longer he waited the greater was the obligation to him; not alone in money; but in forbearance and disinterested generosity. He would not ask to be repaid. He had added to the burden of debt by not expecting thanks or return. Isobel Martin came to a full, perhaps an exaggerated, realisation of the magnitude of this bill with horror. She could not repay it.

To one of Isobel's breed the prospect of remaining under an obligation to anyone who regarded her, as she believed John Harkness did, was shattering to self respect. In that she was as Northern as was John Harkness himself. No personal happiness or comfort or wish could be permitted to lower the standard of what one expected, not so much of oneself, it was bigger than that, but of one's stock; of one's self, not as a person, but as a representative of one's ancestors and descendants.

Reluctantly Isobel allowed her thoughts to turn to Charles. She knew whither they would carry her finally. John Harkness wanted to keep Charles in the firm. He could not buy Charles. Isobel knew that he would willingly pay more to keep Charles than he had paid to assist the children of Hugh Martin. If she gave up Charles she would have squared her account many times over. The money could then be repaid in instalments. She, Isobel, would always be there to see to that. At first as the project took definite shape in her mind, Isobel shrank from it in despair. When she had told Charles, at the Races, that he ought to stay, she had known, known with triumphant happiness, that he would put her before even his father. It was not fair to Charles, she told herself wildly. He, as well as herself, would be paying John Harkness's account. But she loved Charles and he loved her; there was no question of debt or obligation between people who felt for each other as did she and Charles. The fact that her unhappiness must be shared by Charles was inevitable, it did not alter the issue. John Harkness must be paid.

Isobel did not cry herself to sleep that night, as she had done on a previous occasion on deciding that Charles Harkness was not for her. She lay awake and wondered why life was so needlessly long. She might have to live for fifty years still. Fifty years just then seemed a long time to Isobel.

Charles came down to the farm as usual on Saturday afternoon. He seldom saw Isobel, except by special arrangement during the week, but he normally came to Dromara on Saturday and returned to Belfast on Sunday evening. Sometimes he spent the night with Edward, who was still keeping on his house at Ringawoody, but to please Marie, and, he hoped, his father, he more often stayed at 'Craigaveagh'.

His father had seemed almost pathetically pleased to see him on the first occasion he had turned up at home, though since then he had treated his son's visits as a matter of course. Both father and son shrank from having things out. Otherwise, they must long ago have solved, or, finally placed beyond solution, the problem that worried them both. A good row would have cleared the atmosphere, but John Harkness did not believe in having rows, except about comparatively trivial matters.

Charles was thinking of his father a good deal these days. He missed him more than he had thought possible. His new job was interesting, but it was not the same as managing Ringawoody. Charles drove round to the house to leave in his case. He was just as glad his father was not in from the mill as he had promised Isobel that he would try to be early, and he was anxious to get away to Dromara immediately.

Marie, however, intercepted him in the hall. 'Oh, Charles, I'm so glad to see you. I ...' she hesitated. 'I want to tell you something.'

Charles kissed her affectionately. 'You sound excited about it. Has the cat had kittens?'

Marie pushed him away. 'No. You mustn't laugh, Charles. It's very important. Are you taking your case up? I'll come up with you.'

'I wasn't going to take it up,' Charles admitted. 'But come on. We must have privacy for this thrilling story of yours.'

Marie closed the door with elaborate caution. 'You promise you won't tell anyone?' she asked.

'I promise,' Charles said smilingly.

'Honour bright?'

'Honour bright,' he repeated dutifully.

'Charles, I'm going to get married ... next month. We're not going to tell daddy until after. We're going to be married secretly. I'm telling you because I always tell you everything.'

Charles gaped at her. 'Marie, what are you talking about? Are you off your head?'

Marie looked disappointed. 'Why shouldn't I get married as much as you and Isobel?'

Charles, despite his shock, repressed a smile with difficulty. 'Don't be silly! When you are as old as I am we will let you marry as much as you like. Whom were you thinking of marrying by the way?'

'I'm going to marry Peter Montgomery,' said Marie obstinately. 'And I think you are very mean.'

Charles looked grim. 'You have been seeing Peter Montgomery without father's permission?'

Marie moved uneasily. Charles looked a bit like daddy just now. She wished she hadn't told him. 'Yes. Peter was going to ask if we could be engaged, but now he thinks it would be better to get married first and tell him afterwards. Then he can't stop us.'

'I see,' said Charles. 'Peter seems to be a lad of infinite resource. You can tell him now, with my compliments, that the whole thing is off.'

Marie began to see that she was not going to be deprived of her gesture of loyalty after all. She was sorry that the gesture meant a quarrel with Charles. In her secret heart of hearts Marie thought Charles miles above the normal run of brothers. But one had one's own life to live. Marie read a fair amount of modern literature, and she knew that living one's own life meant something important, even if she was not sure what.

'I cannot do that, Charles.' Marie liked the quiet, determined sound of her own voice. It made everything seem so final and slightly sad. 'I've promised to marry Peter, and you see I want to marry him. I've thought it all out, not just now, but months ago.'

Charles lit a cigarette. 'I thought you had a clearer notion of playing the game, Marie. If you're set on marrying Peter Montgomery I don't suppose anyone can prevent you, but you promised me some time ago that you would tell father that you were seeing him. Why did you not keep your word?'

'Peter did not wish it. It was as much his affair as mine. I couldn't spoil his chances like that.'

Charles turned to her angrily. 'That is all he has been thinking about ... his own chances. Marie, can't you see that if he were a man at all he would not wish to drag you into an underhand business like this? Whatever he may or may not be, he's obviously a coward.'

'He's not,' stormed Marie. 'You know nothing about him. You're just a snob, and I don't care what you say, I'm not going to give him up – even if daddy turns me out, and you never speak to me again.'

Charles shook her, almost roughly. 'You're a fool, Marie; a silly, romantic fool. Peter Montgomery is not in love with you. A man in love isn't a coward. He doesn't plan and scheme and think of his chances and himself and everything else, but the girl he's going to marry. That's what Peter has been doing. He wants to marry you because your father owns the mill. I would forgive that if he went about it decently and openly, but he hasn't. If dad turned you out he wouldn't look at you.'

'Charles, you have no right to say that. It's not fair and it's not true. I know Peter has his faults, but I do believe that I mean more to him than anything else. I would ruin his life if

I were to give him up, and I would ruin my own. I'm not going to do it, Charles, not for you or daddy or anyone.'

'I'm sorry, Marie, but I'm afraid that is exactly what you are going to do, until you have had more time to think it over at any rate. The secret wedding is certainly off. We must have Peter in the open and see what stuff is in him. If he's all you imagine there's nothing to fret about.'

'You're going to tell daddy?' said Marie incredulously.

'I certainly am.'

'But you promised ...'

Charles made one last effort and one that cost him a good deal. He found it difficult to regard Marie as anything but a child. He realised for the first time that she was only a few years younger than Isobel. It was no longer possible to treat her as a youngster and expect her to do as she was told. But Charles hated the unfairness of sentimental appeals, being the victim of an unexpressed one himself.

'I made a much more important promise than that, Marie, years ago. I haven't kept it lately but that was because I trusted you to keep your promise. You didn't. But even now if you guarantee not to see Peter Montgomery until you have told father everything I shall not interfere.'

Marie hesitated. 'Very well,' she said. 'You can tell him. But you can also tell him that I've made up my mind. You think you can make me change, and daddy will think the same. But it won't be any use. I won't ever change.'

Charles left his sister and drove straight to the mill. John Harkness was preparing to leave as he arrived.

'You wanted to speak to me on business?' John Harkness enquired.

Charles told him as tactfully as he could. He would have liked to treat the matter as a joke, but he knew that the situation was far from being humorous. Marie had always been obstinate, and he had the gravest fears that in this case she would stick to her guns. He emphasised this point; his father must understand the situation with which he had to deal.

John Harkness did not appear to see the gravity of the affair. 'Well,' he said, when Charles had come to the end of his explanation. 'I don't see that I can do anything about it. Marie is old enough to know her own mind.'

Vaguely, at the back of John Harkness's mind, a warning was sounding. What was it the mad secretary had said? Bend before the winds of adversity! He had tried to force his will on his children. One by one they had left him. Fate had prepared the same trap once more, but he would not step into it again. He had been rash and foolish in his dealing with Charles, when, as it happened, he could have relied on his judgement. His children were not as foolish as he had imagined. Had she kept out of the mill he would not have wished for a more suitable wife for his son than Hugh Martin's daughter. It was not pleasant for John Harkness to be aware that he had slighted a woman of his own class, and, that woman, the daughter of a man for whom he had had the greatest admiration. In his pride and ignorance he had erected an insurmountable barrier between himself and Charles. His attitude had rankled with the girl's uncle, it must rankle infinitely deeper with the girl herself and with Charles. He could do nothing but profit from the bitter experience of his own arrogance. Marie should not be estranged. He would not have chosen Peter Montgomery as a son-in-law, but he would accept the choice.

Charles was too angry to pick his words. 'You intend to give your consent to Marie marrying that upstart?' he asked.

John Harkness regarded him for a moment in silence. 'I am quite convinced that Marie, no less than you, is capable of dispensing with my consent. I do not intend to turn her adrift, if that's what you mean.'

'There's no need to do that,' said Charles hotly. 'You can get rid of young Montgomery. It was sheer madness ever bringing him in here, and as for making him manager. Well, I always thought you had more sense.'

John Harkness smiled bleakly. 'You and I never saw eye to eye, Charles. And I seem to remember that you were always prejudiced against Montgomery. I can't say I altogether share your prejudices. He seems a decent enough young man, and if Marie has made up her mind to marry him I should not imagine that she will be influenced by anything you or I can say. You were not to be influenced yourself.'

He made this last remark with the hope that Charles might give him an opening to withdraw his objections to his own marriage, but Charles was too furious to be aware of anything but his father's apparent inconsistency. In Charles's eyes his father's attitude to Peter Montgomery increased a thousandfold his insult to Isobel.

Charles's carefully controlled temper gave way, and as so often happens, gave way at the wrong time and about a matter only remotely connected with its real cause. 'No, I was not to be influenced, father, but you did not give me the same consideration that you are prepared to extend to Peter Montgomery. You know what he is and where he came from ... and he hasn't got the decency of his own people ... if he had I would not worry. But he's a sham and a fraud. He's made love to Marie and warned her not to tell you. He would have married her secretly had she not chanced to tell me. You consider a cur like that good enough for Marie? Well, I don't, though I never had the nerve to look down on Isobel Martin. It's just as well you got rid of me. I begin to see that we never would have seen eye to eye. I wish you joy of your son-in-law, father. I trust he will compensate you for the inferiority of your daughter-in-law. He will do his best, I'm sure.'

Charles banged out of the office. It was unfortunate for Peter Montgomery that he had chosen this precise moment to come along the passage. He might possibly have been permitted to pass, for Charles was almost unconscious of his surroundings in his wrath, had he passed unobtrusively. But Peter smiled encouragingly and expressed the wholly inaccurate sentiment that he was glad to see Mr Charles.

Charles looked at him malevolently. Some of the hopelessness that had begun to shroud the affair lifted. There was at least one thing he could do. He did it, with all the force of his strong right arm and over a year's active dislike. Peter collected himself from his full-length position on the floor, with the small amount of dignity possible under the circumstances.

'Mr Charles!' he said in surprise. The surprise was genuine.

'Hold your tongue,' said Charles. 'That's just a taste of what you'll get if you go near my sister again. I've been telling my father of the secret wedding arrangements.' He glanced at the door. 'I should not go in there at the moment if I were you.'

Peter moistened his lips nervously and slipped away. A few minutes later, as he was starting his own car, Charles noted, with satisfaction, Montgomery's car heading off speedily in the direction of Downpatrick. He watched the car speculatively. It ought not to be difficult to scare a rat of Peter's breed out of the country. Charles decided to discuss the matter with Isobel, who had quite original ideas sometimes. Half-an-hour later, when he greeted Isobel, Charles perceived that there was a good deal of truth in the adage about troubles not coming singly. Isobel was in no mood to think up useful plans for the departure of Peter Montgomery.

He looked at her doubtfully. 'What's the matter?' he enquired.

Isobel threw herself into his arms and cried heartbrokenly. 'It was your father bought the farm,' she sobbed. 'I won't be able to pay him back for years. I ca ... can't marry you. Isn't it dreadful?'

Charles persuaded her to sit down. 'Now, listen, Isobel, I've just had a row with Marie and one with father, after which I punched Peter Montgomery on the nose. Don't you start. I'd never forgive myself if I were to punch your nose. I might spoil your appearance forever.'

'It wouldn't matter one bit now,' Isobel assured him tearfully. 'I can't marry you and I've got to stay on this dull old farm for fifty years. I wish I'd never been born.'

'It's far too late to do anything about that now,' Charles pointed out reasonably. 'Women will wish for impossibilities. Let's get to the bottom of all this. How do you know my father bought the farm?'

'Uncle David told me. He's known all the time. I think he definitely asked your father at the Races. Oh, there isn't any doubt about it.'

Charles frowned. 'Well, even if he did? You didn't ask him to. You're not even going to benefit. It seems to me that it is a matter for your uncle and your sisters. You are leaving the place and you have no right to lay down what they ought to do.'

'Tessie and Bridgit are too young to understand, and it's not Uncle David's responsibility. The farm was bought for us. I can't get out of it like that, Charles.'

'Out of what?' said Charles. 'Isobel, you're making a fuss about nothing.'

The girl rose and paced the room in her agitation. With a clearness that startled the man she exposed her pride and resentment and her strangely logical sense of justice. To Charles, smarting from his father's apparent unfairness, her outlook was all too comprehensible. Almost from the beginning of their acquaintance there had existed a mental sympathy between him and Isobel that made ordinary explanations unnecessary. He remembered their strange courtship. Isobel was naturally inclined to be shy and nervous, but she never had been doubtful of him. He knew from experience that girls were easily offended by his flippant tongue, but he had never been afraid of offending Isobel. There had been a sense of exultation in recognising the subtle affinity that existed between them.

That affinity revealed to him now the nature of the struggle that had driven the girl to the desperate step of destroying her own happiness. But he must not listen lest her arguments swayed him in spite of himself. This foolish worship of pride blighted love and kindness and every generous human impulse; and it masqueraded as a virtue. It inevitably claimed as its devotees the straightest and noblest. It had no use for the liar and the rogue. It crept in as self respect, but it ruled as egoism and selfishness disguised in the robe of altruism. Even as he struggled towards what he believed to be the truth, Charles was conscious that Isobel had hesitatingly accompanied him.

He held her closely, tenderly, even as he wounded her without mercy. 'It's pride, Isobel, selfish, personal pride. You hate my father and you cannot bear that you, Isobel Martin, should be under the slightest obligation to him.'

'I don't hate him, Charles,' she said. 'Not now ... He must be kind or he would not have done what he did. But he would rather lose you than let you marry me. That shows what he thinks of me. Charles, I could not owe him anything.'

Charles watched her thoughtfully. 'You need not owe him anything. I'll see that he is paid for the farm.'

'But I'd still owe him something,' said Isobel. 'Can't you see?'

Charles nodded. 'Yes, I see. You would still owe him for the wish to do you and your sisters a kindness?'

'I suppose so,' admitted the girl doubtfully. It seemed all very trivial as Charles put it.

'You decide to do him a kindness,' continued Charles now half-smiling, 'by giving him back something he has never lost, and which actually does not belong to you.'

Isobel twinkled the least little bit. 'Of course, if you're going to be nasty about it ...'

'I think I have every reason to be nasty,' Charles informed her. 'I don't like being exchanged for a dull old farm. In any case I doubt if my father would thank you for the bargain. He made it perfectly plain today that he does not want me back. His objection to you was only a side issue. That side of things does not weigh with him nearly as much as we imagined.'

Isobel sensed the bitterness in his tone. 'Why, Charles? What makes you say that?'

'He is quite prepared to allow Marie to marry Peter Montgomery. So much for his conservatism! If you must pay back for the intention as well as the money you will have to think out another scheme, I'm afraid.'

Isobel sighed. 'I don't care what you say, Charles, you're wrong about your father. He does want you back. I know he does.'

'He can go on wanting. Until today I hoped that in time he would see that he had been unjust, and we might come to some arrangement. After his cool acceptance of Montgomery, I can only think that you had practically nothing to do with his resentment against me. I could not possibly make any suggestion of returning now.'

'Yet you had the cheek to lecture me about pride!' the girl reminded him.

Charles smiled ruefully. 'No,' he said gravely. 'I am really doing my father the good turn you imagine you owe him. My father knows perfectly well that I would have preferred to remain in Ringawoody. Even now I expect I could patch things up and return, without any tragic sacrifices. It is not pride that prevents me. You said that my father must be kind to have done what he did about David Martin's farm. You don't know anything about him. He's fearfully decent. I think a tremendous lot of him. I was sick about this because I was not sure what he really wanted ... and that's about the last thing dad will ever tell you, especially in a personal matter. But, quite honestly, I am pretty sure of my ground now. If I could be like Edward and appear to agree with him in everything it would work grand. It wasn't you that led to the break, it was the fact that I opposed him. That issue is much older and more vital. The other did not really signify. You see he takes a much more unsuitable marriage quite calmly. I am sure that he does not know that he was relieved to be rid of me. I quite believe that he thinks he is sorry. He is sorry in one way, but not in a way that matters very much. He will be much happier on his own.'

Isobel considered the matter doubtfully. It sounded convincing, but her intuition told her that there was something wrong somewhere. She knew that Charles was bitterly disappointed, and she did her best to cheer him. 'You're as bad as your father,' she said flippantly. 'If I had half the bees the Harknesses have in their bonnets I could make a fortune selling honey. But what's all this about Peter Montgomery and Marie?'

Charles's gloom rapidly changed to indignation as he outlined the story. To whatever he may have resigned himself he certainly had not resigned himself to Peter Montgomery as a husband for Marie. 'Dad cannot possibly realise what a little toad he is,' he said furiously. 'That sham polish of his always gave me the pip. I know he's crooked and an absolute swine, and Marie is such a nice kid. I'd rather see her dead ... But it's going to be stopped, if I have to knock the blighter's head off.'

'That is one way of settling it, certainly,' agreed Isobel, who was inclined to the opinion that the knocking off of Peter Montgomery's head would be no great loss to the country. However, with feminine conservatism she was in favour of taking a middle course. 'I can't stand the creature myself, and I don't know what Marie sees in him. But women fall in love with the most unprepossessing specimens. I suppose I can't afford to talk,' and she smiled teasingly at Charles.

'Don't waste your intelligence trying to be witty,' he expostulated. 'This is serious. Think of something. I'm sure there's lots of incriminating evidence against him if we could only get hold of it. And one point in his favour is that he'd run for next to nothing. He hasn't the guts of a snipe.'

'Never mind the details,' said Isobel. 'Stick to the broad outline. Had you anything against him at the mill?'

Charles kicked a chair savagely. 'Nothing definite. But I didn't trust him, and he knew it. He took good care to cover his tracks when I was round. I know he's swindling the firm. You've only got to look at him to know that he's a born swindler.'

'That kind of evidence isn't entirely conclusive,' Isobel pointed out. 'If you hinted anything like that to your father he would probably ignore it; and, if he took it seriously, and Peter was able to clear himself, he'd have a stronger position with your father than ever.'

'Oh, I know. Dad always liked him; he's as simple as a child. I don't think he could believe that any employee of Harkness's would be capable of dishonesty.'

'You evidently do not agree with him?' laughed Isobel.

'Not as far as Montgomery is concerned. That lad is not capable of honesty. He's so darned crooked he'd probably break his back if he tried to straighten himself.'

'I like his sister,' said Isobel.

'So do I. I liked the whole family. But things like Peter might happen in any family. I'm sorry for his mother and sisters, but I'm hanged if I'm going to have him messing up our family. It would be bad enough if Marie was one of those aggressive, domineering females who could wipe the floor with him, but she's a sentimental idealist; he'd break her heart.'

Isobel sat up. 'Talking about wiping the floor with him reminds me of Nancy. She can handle him.' She sprang to her feet excitedly. 'Charles, I believe we've got it. Nancy is devoted to Marie. She's been like a hen with one chick about her since that time Marie fell off the horse.'

'But Peter happens to be Nancy's brother,' said Charles doubtfully. 'And, anyway, I don't see that she can do anything.'

'Nancy Orr could do anything she set her mind to,' said Isobel confidently. 'Helen of Troy, Cleopatra and the Queen of Sheba were only trotting after Nancy for genuine strength of character. If Peter can be scared into showing a clean pair of heels Nancy can do the job, and I believe she would. She has no very high opinion of her superior brother.'

'But Marie wouldn't thank her if she did interfere,' said Charles, as though determined to see the dark side.

Isobel laughed. 'Nancy is not the kind to look for thanks if she thought she was doing Marie a good turn. She'd enjoy the excitement. I'm going to see her, Charles; if I can't exchange you for the farm, perhaps I can save your father from Peter Montgomery.'

'It's Marie I'm worrying about,' said Charles.

'It's all the same,' said Isobel impatiently. 'You Harknesses are like the Clan McTavish, only stickier. Will you help me on with my coat and stop looking like somebody's funeral?'

CHAPTER ELEVEN

Nancy had just returned from Belfast when Isobel and Charles arrived. Though her mother had been very ill, Nancy's statements to Peter, regarding the exact degree of danger, were something of an exaggeration. But in spite of the fact that Mrs Montgomery was now well on the road to recovery, Nancy was in anything but a placid humour. She had learned from her mother that Peter had not kept his word. Nancy had come to accept the breaking of Peter's promises as part of the natural order of the day, but her mother's grief and disappointment distressed her. The memory of the pain in the sick woman's eyes, when she had heard that her son had neglected her after being told that she was dying, made Nancy want to do something violent.

'I wish he'd get smallpox,' she fumed. 'Sure all yon vaccination was the greatest mistake at all.'

The stage was thus carefully set for the business Charles and Isobel had in view. Charles decided that Isobel had better do the talking. He did not wish to hurt Nancy's feelings by the terms in which he felt bound to refer to her brother. On that particular score he need not have worried himself. Nancy could improve on anyone's description of her only masculine relative.

Isobel began cautiously. She explained that she had nothing against Peter. Furthermore, Mr Harkness thought highly of him, but Marie was very young for such a grave step, and naturally her family did not approve of Peter's idea of a secret wedding. Isobel had seen Nancy simmering; she had also seen her boil over, but she had never seen her as angry as she was now. It is difficult to credit, but for some time Nancy was speechless with rage. When she found her voice, it seemed that the one she found was hardly her own. It sounded strange and flat.

'And what does John Harkness say to this?' she asked.

Charles answered her. 'My father is agreeable. He thinks that Marie is old enough to know her own mind.'

'Has he told Peter the same?'

Charles smiled grimly. 'Not yet. Peter left hurriedly after he had seen me.'

'Aye, he would,' said Nancy. 'But he'll go further and in a bigger hurry before I've finished with him.'

'Can you do anything, Nancy?' asked Isobel eagerly.

'Maybe,' said Nancy. 'I must think. Would you like a cup of tea?'

'No, no. Never mind the tea. Think!'

But Nancy insisted on making tea. She brought out her scones, her oatcakes and her fruit loaf. She pressed pancakes and potato bread on her visitors as though the glorification of her own cooking were the only concern she had in the world. When her guests were fed she chatted pleasantly about Frank, her mother and her young ducklings. She told the story of Rosie and the silk stockings. In spite of their anxiety Isobel and Charles found themselves listening to her humorous account with interest and laughing heartily over Marie's predicament. Several hours passed in cheerful aimless chatter.

At length Nancy looked at the clock and rose. 'I'm thinking John Harkness will have finished his dinner by now. I have business with him. Maybe you would be good enough to run me along to 'Craigaveagh', Mr Charles?' she said quietly.

Charles agreed, frankly puzzled.

'I thought you would see Peter?' said Isobel, who was equally bewildered.

'What made you think the like of that?' replied Nancy as she departed to don her Sunday coat. Whatever she might say of John Harkness, Nancy always paid him the tribute of dressing up for an interview with him. Nancy knew what was owing to the Head of Ringawoody Spinning Mill. She might modify, but she would never entirely discard the counsel of her mother. Nancy had been brought up to obey her parents, love God, and honour the King. This included wearing her Sunday coat at Church and on other solemn or important occasions. There is a fundamental soundness in people who have Sunday coats.

Isobel looked questioningly at Charles. 'What *is* she going to do?'

Charles shrugged. 'Search me! But I'm beginning to have confidence in Nancy. She has a look about her.'

'Hush!' whispered Isobel. 'She's coming. I wish I had her courage.'

Charles looked at her curiously, but said nothing. Isobel flushed. She was perfectly aware of exactly what he had not said. Nancy joined them and the three drove to 'Craigaveagh.'

'Would you like me to come in with you?' Charles asked.

Nancy shook her head. 'I'll go my lone,' she said, and before Charles could make further suggestions or enquiries she walked up to the front door and rang the bell.

Charles would have followed her but Isobel laid a restraining hand on his arm. 'Wait,' she said urgently. 'Let her manage it in her own way.'

'But we can't sit here like a pair of fools,' said Charles.

'We'll go on to Dromara,' said Isobel calmly. 'I'm sure Nancy knows what she is about, and we can't do anything more now. You can come straight back for her when you leave me home.'

After a moment's hesitation Charles started the car.

John Harkness had dined alone in his study. He did so to avoid a discussion with Marie. He had resigned himself to her marriage with Peter Montgomery, but he was anxious to postpone the granting of his consent as long as possible. He told himself that he desired time to think the matter over calmly. As he stared at the fire he realised morosely that there was nothing to think about. He had already considered Charles's suggestion that he should rid himself of Montgomery, but he had come to the conclusion that such a step would but increase Marie's determination to marry him. He had no legitimate excuse for dismissing the young man. It was out of the question. A maid came to the door.

'There is a Mrs Orr wishes to see you, sir.'

'Mrs Orr?' John Harkness frowned, then remembered Nancy Montgomery. He was conscious of a slight sense of shock as he recalled that a previous meeting with Nancy had led indirectly to his present trouble. What was it Charles had said about smiling on Peter because he had frowned on Paul?

'Show her in,' he said to the maid.

As Nancy entered John Harkness rose and bowed gravely. 'Can I be of service to you, Mrs Orr?' he enquired politely.

Nancy turned away from the seat he indicated. 'No, Mr Harkness, you can be of no service to me. You could no see your way to be of service to me when I asked you. Maybe it sounds strange, but I come tonight to try to do you a service. It's a brave long road as has no turning.'

'I am afraid I do not quite understand,' said the man patiently. 'Has your visit any connection with your brother?'

'Aye,' said Nancy, 'it has so. I hear he's for marrying your daughter, Mr Harkness?'

John Harkness looked at her cautiously. 'And of what service can you be in the matter?' he asked.

'Maybe you're no so dead set against the wedding?' said Nancy. 'Peter is a nice-spoken lad, and it could be he has got round you. Peter was aye able to get round a fool.'

'I have nothing against your brother,' said John Harkness, ignoring her last remark.

Nancy's excitement was gradually growing. 'Are you standing there, Mr Harkness, and telling me ye'd let your wee girl marry a rat like Peter Montgomery?'

The man started, but he hastily covered his surprise. 'I'm afraid I shall have very little say in the matter.' Even as he spoke, he knew that she had more to say – if she would say it.

'You had plenty to say about Mr Charles. Everybody knows you turned him out because he wanted to marry Isobel Martin. Who were you, John Harkness, to look down on Hugh Martin's daughter? When you have a record as long as the Martins you will no need to be giving so much attention to your dignity; it will grow without attention. And then you turn round and are willing to take in a scamp like that brother of mine. Are you right in the head, man?'

'You are speaking of the manager of my mill. You appear to have nothing against him but your own dislike? He may be your brother, but I cannot permit you to discuss him before me in such terms,' said John Harkness coldly.

Nancy laughed. It was not a particularly pleasant laugh. 'Nothing against him! If I was to stand here till the morrow morning, I could no get through the half of what I've against Peter Montgomery – no, nor the quarter. An' it was no for your innocent wee lassie I'd let you find out all you could about me grand brother.'

John Harkness sat down. 'Please sit down, Mrs Orr,' he said gently.

Nancy sat down mechanically.

'Now I am quite sure you mean well,' he continued. 'I, naturally, have the happiness of my daughter very much at heart. She wishes to marry your brother, and unless you have definite reasons why she should not do so, any interference of mine would be useless. Merely calling him a "scamp" and a "rat" is beside the point. You must have reasons for thinking so badly of him. You say you came to do me a service. I appreciate your intention, but why not be perfectly frank with me?'

Nancy had no shred of loyalty left for her brother. Yet, when it came to the point of placing him in actual danger of the law she shrank from the task. But she could not let him marry Marie Harkness ... Marle had almost taken the place of Nancy's dead baby in her heart.

'I will tell you, but I must think of my mother. It would kill her if Peter was put in prison ... you will let him have the chance to leave the country?'

John Harkness looked grave. 'Prison? Nancy, do you realise what you are saying?'

'God help me! I do,' said Nancy. 'You will let him go, sir?'

'If it be in my power,' said John Harkness.

As Nancy told of her suspicions at the time of the deficit when William Davidson's insanity had been discovered, John Harkness's face darkened. If this were true, he, himself had largely assisted in covering up the fraud. Mr Grey, Edward and Charles had all pressed for a more thorough investigation at the time. But it had seemed so unnecessary, and he had been unwilling to bring the details of the poor, unfortunate, lunatic's folly to light.

'Have you anything but your own suspicion to back the suggestion that Peter was implicated?' he asked.

'Yes. But just little things. Peter lied to me. He knew rightly I suspected him. He said as there was no money missing. He'd moved to the hotel in Downpatrick, he'd bought a car and was running all over the country in it. He was no doing that on his salary.'

'And since then? You think ...'

'I know he's robbing you blind. He wanted my mother out of the place, and he bought a house in Belfast. He bought two houses. He said as he borrowed the money off the bank. He explained all about it being easy to borrow money to buy houses. I might have believed him had he no done so much explaining. Peter only explains when he's lying. You see I know him – he never was no good. Peter's no happy unless he's cheating somebody ... It is a queer, strange thing, for he's terrible feared of being found out.'

John Harkness was slow to accept an unsupported accusation, but, he recognised the damning significance of Nancy's scrappy evidence. It was possible that she was mistaken, but there was no doubt that she, herself, was firmly convinced of her brother's guilt. In her knowledge of him she had observed details that might have been passed over by others; but, in the light of circumstances, those details carried conviction. He turned to her now as a man might seek advice from an intelligent friend. 'I hardly know what to think, Nancy. What you say certainly rouses my gravest suspicions, but even if all this is true and could be proved, I doubt if Marie could be convinced of Peter's guilt.'

Nancy nodded slowly. 'There's that. And even if she was she might stick to him all the more. Womenfolk is queer. He'd have some grand long tale for her you may be sure, and she'd believe him. A woman can aye believe what she likes to think is true.' She paused and looked thoughtfully at the fire. The man said nothing; for the moment he had fallen under the spell of Nancy's dominating efficiency. 'I thought of a way this evening.' She opened her bag and produced a roll of notes. 'There's fifty pounds here; it's to pay Peter's fare to ... wherever he takes the notion to go.'

'But,' began John Harkness.

Nancy interrupted him as though she were flicking aside an annoying fly. 'You must no say anything to Marie or to Peter. Peter will be angry with her for telling Mr Charles, but if he knew he was suspected of the other he'd get over his anger brave and fast, so let that be. Peter has taken to the drink lately, and unless I'm far out he is no easy in his mind. You have a new secretary in, and you can say as you are having a special counting up of the books and things so as he can get the right hold of things.'

John Harness listened approvingly. 'As a matter of fact had I not been so busy something of the sort would have been done a week ago. Your brother is still more or less doing the two jobs, which is unsatistactory.'

Nancy smiled. 'I think so too. When you've counted up maybe you'll see how unsatisfactory.'

The man looked uneasy. The thought of almost open dishonesty going on in his own mill under his own eyes annoyed him intensely as reflecting on his own supervision. 'It is possible that you are quite mistaken,' he said somewhat testily.

'Aye, and it's possible that pigs might fly. You can take it from me that so be you give Peter warning he will no wait for the counting.'

John Harkness was relieved and concerned at the same time. If Peter Montgomery took himself off there was no doubt that the situation would be eased considerably. Marie could not blame him for the uneasy conscience of the young man, and he was quite within his rights to call in the auditors at any time. But John Harkness disliked the suggestion of a plot; he also strongly objected to giving countenance to any scheme to cheat the law. 'The whole thing is most irregular,' he said dubiously.

Nancy had no use for such finicky nonsense. 'You promised that he would no go to prison if it was in your power to let him go. You must abide by that. If he's guilty you're well rid of him; if ...' Nancy stressed the word with infinite sarcasm, 'he's no, there's no harm done.'

'Very well,' said John Harkness. 'It shall be as you say. Whatever may come of it I am deeply grateful for your concern regarding my daughter.'

Nancy rose brusquely. 'I want none of your gratitude,' she said ungraciously. 'As things turned out well for me I bear you no ill will, but I owe you nothing, and I want nothing of you.' She placed the notes which she had taken from her bag, on the table. 'Maybe you would be good enough to ask Peter to put this in the bank – after you tell him about the counting up. I have a notion he will know what to do with it, under the circumstances. It's the only gift I'd give Peter Montgomery, with a glad heart, as you might say.'

John Harkness smiled at her admiringly. 'No, Nancy. You must allow me the privilege of paying my manager's fare, should his hasty departure materialise.'

'I am sure you would no grudge it,' agreed Nancy. 'But it's what my mother would want done. She aye had the great notion of family pride ... I'd have paid for his funeral decent-like, and this is the next best thing.'

The man held out his hand hardly knowing whether to be shocked or amused. 'You have a bitter tongue, Nancy. But one could wish that your brother were more like you.'

Nancy shook hands awkwardly. 'You were no of that opinion always,' she said dourly. 'Goodnight to you!'

John Harkness saw her to the door and observed that Charles's car was waiting. He reflected guiltily that Charles had always been distrustful of Montgomery. He had probably persuaded Nancy to the final step of betraying her brother. Charles's resentment had not been pure prejudice; without knowing the actual facts, he had nevertheless, recognised young Montgomery as untrustworthy. He had stressed the point frequently, and, as had so often been the case, he was right. He considered his son's talents gloomily. Charles was lost to Ringawoody.

CHAPTER TWELVE

While Nancy was engaged in shattering her brother's prospects in John Harkness's study, the victim of her efforts was cursing women in general, and Marie Harkness in particular, as untrustworthy chatterers of whom all ambitious and progressive young men should steer clear. Peter had little hopes now of retaining his position. He interpreted Charles's attack as indicating the general opinion of the Harkness family, or at least those members of it who were of any importance. He had worked and sweated and planned, to be undone, when victory was in sight, by the tongue of an idiotic girl. He had been a fool to trust her. He might have known ... He had returned to Ringawoody with the half-formed notion of seeing Mr Harkness and promising to break with Marie. There was a faint chance that if he came forward at once with such an offer ... and he could, of course, deny any story of a secret marriage having been arranged; he might make it appear that the whole thing had been a kind of distant worship on his part, and that he had never presumed to look for serious favour from the daughter of his employer ... It was just possible that he might yet save his job.

But when he reached the drive which led up to 'Craigaveagh' his courage deserted him. Awe of John Harkness was rooted deeply in him, reaching far beneath the glib, polished exterior which hid from undiscriminating eyes the pitiable creature that was Peter Montgomery. He found his suave excuses and explanations leaving him; the speech he had planned seemed inadequate. He turned his car. He would put off the meeting until the morning; better practise his opening better. A favourable beginning counted for a good deal; just to hit the right note ... he could not afford to blunder. By morning he would be more composed. At the moment he was too angry; temper might prove fatal. He had been foolish to drink that brandy ... drink made him indiscreet. At this point in his cogitations he caught sight of the cause of all his trouble walking briskly towards him. Marie, finding the evening dull had brought out her favourite spaniel for a walk. When she saw Peter's car she waved joyfully. Peter stopped and got out. At least he had no fear of Marie. She offered herself as an excellent outlet for his rage. He welcomed the opportunity of revenge, and it were as well to let her know plainly how things stood. Marie's radiant smile and shining eyes infuriated the man. The stupid, little fool didn't realise that she had landed him in a mess! She must be half-witted.

'I'm so glad I met you,' said Marie eagerly. 'I've something to tell you.'

'And I've something to tell you, my lady,' said Peter savagely. 'You've cost me my job with that clattering tongue of yours.'

'Peter!' Marie was too amazed to be angry.

'For God's sake give it over! I've put up with your damn fool nonsense long enough. Who do you think you are, anyway? I suppose you imagined I was flattered by your simpering notice ...' He laughed harshly.

Marie was trembling with terror. She was quite sure that Peter had gone mad like poor Mr Davidson. It must be something about the mill. The managers all seemed to go queer. She pulled herself together bravely.

'Don't you feel well?' she enquired nervously

Peter shrugged his despair of her. 'Shut up, you fool! If you talked less you wouldn't have got me into this mess. What did you want to tell your father about us for? Didn't I warn you to hold your tongue?'

Marie stiffened. 'I did not tell father. I told Charles. I had to tell Charles, and Charles made me let him tell daddy.'

'Oh, I see,' snarled Peter. 'The good little girl had to tell her big brother, and he had to tell her daddy. Wasn't that just too sweet!'

Marie fushed angrily. 'Aren't you being rather ... uncouth?' she said disdainfully. His taunting sneer had banished the child in her.

'Oh yes, my lady. I'm much too uncouth for you now that your stuck-up family are down on me.'

'You will please refrain from discussing my family,' said Marie with increasing calm. 'They do not come into this. This is a matter between you and me.'

'Is it?' said Peter. 'Well, I can tell you that any matter between you and me is finished. Do you think I'd tie myself up to an idiot who can't hold her tongue for five minutes. I shall see your father in the morning and tell him I'm through with you.'

'Thanks Peter, that will save me the trouble. I am sure my father will be relieved. Come here, Pat!' she turned to call the dog.

Something in her tone and bearing robbed the man of his last vestige of control. Though he had aped her class, he hated and envied it. He knew that he lacked the training that might have given his careful imitation the appearance of being genuine. Knowing his own limitations he regarded the girl's composure as a personal insult. His revenge had fallen flat. Beside himself now with sheer unrestrained temper he snatched the little switch from her hand and struck her savagely. Pat rushed up growling ominously. Marie stepped back quickly and grasped the dog's lead. Peter dropped the switch in consternation. For once in his life, he was shocked by his own behaviour.

'I didn't mean to do that,' he said sullenly.

Marie glanced at him over her shoulder. She laughed, the merest chuckle of amusement. 'Not just uncouth ...' she said lightly. 'Positively primitive. Goodnight, Montgomery. You really ought to join our Temperance Association, we've had some marvellous cures.'

As she coaxed Pat up the drive and tried to assure him that Peter Montgomery was not at all a suitable meal for a thoroughbred dog, Marie was inclined to the opinion that her own cure was even more marvellous than anything the Temperance Association had achieved.

'I think it must be only on the Pictures that girls really appreciate these playful taps,' she explained to herself good-humouredly. For a girl who had been so cruelly jilted and disillusioned, she was disgustingly cheerful, but she had just remembered that now she need not have a lifelong quarrel with Charles, and the question of her being turned adrift by an irate parent would not arise. Everything has its compensations.

Peter was given no opportunity to announce his renunciation of Marie to John Harkness. The Head of the Firm did not put in an appearance the next day until late in the afternoon, and when he did so his first remarks to his manager put all thoughts of keeping his job out of that young man's head.

'I have been in Belfast, Montgomery,' he said conversationally. 'And, by the way, I have asked Mr Grey to come down in the morning. I want Henderson to take complete charge in the office from now on. We've been rather confused since that sad affair of Davidson, but it's time we were back to our old routine. Have the books ready for Mr Grey in the morning.'

Had he entertained any doubts, the sudden pallor that masked Montgomery's face would have convinced John Harkness of the truth of Nancy's accusation. He looked contemptuously at the abject fear in Peter's eyes. He felt tired and rather sick. The whole business nauseated him.

Peter was about to leave the room.

'Come here,' said John Harkness sternly.

Peter turned, but he did not look at his employer.

'The books are *not* right?' said John Harkness.

Peter looked round him like a trapped animal. In his terror and misery he looked pathetically young.

Few men can look on a criminal, especially a young criminal, faced with the consequence of his crimes, with any degree of satisfaction. The important fact that one has been the victim of dishonesty seems to lose its significance in the tragedy of it all. The sense of elation, that one ought quite justifiably be able to experience is strangely absent; instead there is embarrassment and an inexplicable feeling of shame, as though one were somehow responsible.

John Harkness regarded the youth frowningly ... He was a mere boy. Dishonest, without doubt, but far too young to have been entrusted with such responsibility. Lacking background and training he had been unable to resist the temptation of the opportunities his position had given him. The man reflected that his own action was almost as criminal as the lad's. In that moment he was glad that his promise to Nancy prevented the sordid little tragedy from dragging to an otherwise inevitable end in a Court of Law, with a long sentence of imprisonment looming in the background.

'Have you any idea of the sum involved?' he asked quietly.

Peter swayed unsteadily. 'Nearly a thousand pounds,' he said thickly.

John Harkness shook his head. 'You fool,' he said. 'You young fool. You must have known that you would be found out sooner or later?'

'I intended to put things right,' said Peter.

'That is the distant intention of most people like you, Montgomery, but the intention, unfortunately, becomes increasingly distant. Such intentions carry very little weight with a judge.'

Peter grasped the desk in his terror. 'You are going to give me in charge?' he gasped.

John Harkness rose. 'No, Montgomery. I ought to notify the police but your sister intervened on your behalf. I shall make no charge provided you clear out immediately.'

A venomous expression crept into Peter's face. 'Nancy gave me away?'

'Nancy knew what was coming and saved you from prison,' said John Harkness harshly. His sympathy for the young man was waning.

'Oh, I'll get out,' said Peter. 'The whole thing is a put-up job.'

'If you remain in the country after the end of the week you will be arrested. I hope that is perfectly plain. You will be well advised to hasten your departure as much as possible. I may say that I am inclined to regret my leniency already.'

Peter cringed again. 'I'm sorry, sir. I hardly know what I'm saying. You have shown great forbearance – more than I deserve.'

'You deserve none. I can only express the hope that this will be a lesson to you. Have you any money?'

Peter looked at him cautiously. 'A little – enough for my fare,' he added hastily.

John Harkness wrote a cheque. 'Part of this is a gift from your sister. She was anxious that you should be allowed to get away safely. See you go quickly. Your safety depends largely upon your speed. That is all.'

Peter Montgomery went, a disheartened young man, who considered himself badly used by a world that made no allowances for ambitious and progressive young men.

He goes out of our story and we hear of him but once again, and that, indirectly.

When he was going over his cheques returned from the bank at a later date, John Harkness came across one made payable to Mr Peter Montgomery; the sum was £400. John Harkness had every reason to remember this particular cheque, which in point of fact had been made payable for €100. His improvement on Nancy's plan had cost him £300. But his preference for acting on his own discretion had often cost him much more.

Spring gave place to Summer. Roses came out in the Ringawoody loanings. Visitors came to the Spa. The Mill Row brought up the old grievance of absent bathrooms, more from principle than any definite sense of necessity; there was the faintest tinge of mild Socialism in Ringawoody. There was also the annual water shortage, due, the villagers declared, to the enormous export of County Down water from the Silent Valley to Belfast. What had caused the shortage before the Silent Valley Water Scheme was set up, being very ancient history, was naturally not discussed. One is inclined to the view that the local County Councils were not entirely blameless.

Nancy Orr certainly held that view. She even went so far as to write a very stiff letter to the *Down Recorder* on the subject. The letter was mentioned at a meeting of the County Council in Downpatrick, and several people said that something ought to be done. It was not right that people should pay water rates when taps and pumps functioned spasmodically or not at all. However, June gave way to the customary wet July, and most of the arguments in favour of more water began to look absurd. Anyway the question had taken on a political and religious significance involving the Ulster Prime Minister and the Catholic Minority, and it was about time the Heavens intervened.

Ringawoody Spinning Mill clacked on monotonously. Prophesied linen booms failed to come up to expectations, but linen continued to improve, gradually, if unspectacularly. Harkness's were kept busy spinning yarn. No new manager had been appointed. With the expense of Peter Montgomery and the mortgage incurred over Edward's withdrawal, the firm had come through an unprofitable year. John Harkness decided to manage the mill himself. He assured himself that he did so in the interests of economy. There was time enough. He could make a permanent appointment later. Charles and Isobel were married early in June. It was a big wedding, as they were both well-known. John Harkness attended the church ceremony, but he avoided receptions or anything of a social nature.

'He evidently does not intend to come round,' remarked Charles.

Isobel said nothing. Her debt to John Harkness still rankled despite the fact that Charles had faithfully promised that it should be paid.

During her honeymoon, and for the first few months of her married life, Isobel thrust aside all thought of John Harkness. With a new house, a new husband, and a constant succession of new maids she found her life sufficiently full to exclude all doubts and uncertainties. But even after a wedding, life must readjust itself, and, sooner or later normal routine set in. In time Isobel found herself with a competent maid and a good deal of spare time on her hands. She was very happy with Charles. She was also an intelligent, sensible girl not in the least given to interpreting a long afternoon as a sign that her husband no longer loved her; nor yet as evidence that she was suffering from the Hollywood epidemic of Incompatibility of Temperament – that imaginary, but incurable disease bred of lack of resource and a surfeit of spare time. She saw many interesting possibilities in her new life in Belfast, but she missed her old friends and her old environment; from her own sense of loss she calculated Charles's.

The break with Ringawoody had widened since the wedding. Isobel had not been invited to 'Craigaveagh.' She would have gone willingly with Charles had he made the suggestion, but he did not do so. He read the omission as another slight on his wife, or, at least, as an expression of his father's determination to ignore her existence. Relations between father and son had been strained since Charles's outburst in the office. John Harkness's bare recognition of the wedding had not helped, with the result that Charles had not visited his home since his marriage. Isobel knew that he was not entirely happy. He could not be drawn into an unguarded remark where Ringawoody was concerned; to one who understood him as did Isobel no amount of reserve could quite conceal the wound he would have hidden even from himself.

'It's a pity to spoil two houses with those two men. They're undoubtedly chips off the same obstinate block,' Isobel thought to herself, with tender amusement, one morning at breakfast when Charles, after reading a letter from Marie with obvious eagerness, laid it aside with assumed indifference.

'Any news?' she enquired.

'Oh, no. Just Marie's usual chatter. She is coming up to town this afternoon. She'll probably be round. Keep her until I get home. I haven't seen her for ages.'

'She usually goes home on the four bus, the later one is always crowded. Of course you could easily run her home ... She is nervous driving in the city.'

'Never mind,' said Charles carelessly. 'I'll see her some other time. Remember me to her.'

'I don't think she's at all likely to forget you, Charles,' said Isobel a little unsteadily.

He touched her hand; for a moment she caught his old, intimate, quizzical smile. 'Don't worry yourself, Isobel,' he said rising. 'In-laws are always indigestible.'

After he had gone Isobel sat and considered the situation. If Charles and his father were really alike, it was perfectly ridiculous to be afraid of John Harkness. Vaguely, but with gradually increasing misgivings, she realised that her fear, with the nervous resentment that had grown from it, had been largely to blame for the present position. She had been given ample opportunities, but, she had somehow always bungled them. Instead of behaving in a natural and friendly manner she had shown antagonism. Even Charles had said that she could get on with his father, if she wanted to. She had not wanted to. In a moment of that stark honesty, of which few feminine minds are capable, she knew that almost unconsciously, she had wished to separate Charles from his father and all that claimed him at Ringawoody. She had neither planned nor schemed, but, she had moved steadily, almost involuntarily towards her goal.

The thought of approaching her father-in-law returned and was rejected in panic many times in the course of the day. It could do no good now and Charles would be angry. A thousand excuses came readily enough. But the thought crept back. It could do no harm. Should nothing come of it she need not tell Charles. It were pointless to distress him unnecessarily. She would do anything for Charles – almost anything; and she owed something vague and unsatisfactory to John Harkness.

Marie called and was full of enquiries for Charles. As usual she did not mention her father. Marie had accepted the, to her, strange fact that Isobel did not like him.

Today, Isobel mentioned him herself. 'Do you think your father misses Charles?' she asked bluntly.

Marie was unprepared for so direct an attack. For a moment Isobel thought she was going to cry. 'Dreadfully!'

she stammered. 'Isobel, do you think they will ever make friends?'

Isobel laid a comforting hand on her shoulder. 'Of course. Do you think your father would mind if I went to see him?'

Marie sprang to her feet eagerly. 'Isobel! Would you? I'm quite sure you could make everything all right. I can't bear to see daddy looking so closed-up.'

Isobel laughed nervously. 'If he puts me out I shall blame you,' she warned,

Isobel left an unilluminating message for Charles to the effect that she was going out. As she delivered it she felt that she had foolishly signed her own death warrant. But there was no escape now. Marie hastened the moment of departure in a manner that appeared to her sister-in-law to be utterly indecent. On the way down in the bus the younger girl chattered incessantly; Isobel had a strong inclination to box her ears. She restrained it. After all, Marie was not responsible for her, Isobel's, extraordinary notion to beard sinister monsters in their dens. She looked out of the window and tried Charles's plan of repeating all the poems she knew. She found she knew remarkably few for recitation purposes and had to fall back on the Psalms. From these it was an easy step to Daniel. She found herself thinking of Daniel a good deal.

Finally they reached 'Craigaveagh.'

'Is Mr Harkness at home?' Marie enquired of the maid.

'Yes, Miss, he has just come in.'

To Isobel the undoubted fact that fate had suddenly taken a personal spite against her seemed unfair, but she followed Marie to her father's study.

'Tomorrow it will be over,' she reminded herself. She had found this line of argument cheering as a small child faced with a visit to the dentist. As a reasonable, grown woman faced with a visit to her father-in-law she found no comfort in the thought. Tomorrow meant no more to Isobel, at the moment, than next Christmas means to a White Cabbage Butterfly.

Marie opened the study door as though it were a very ordinary door in an ordinary house. 'Daddy, this is Isobel come to see you,' she said, then she smiled cheerfully at Isobel and left her to her fate. It seemed incredible that anyone so young as Marie could be so completely unscrupulous.

John Harkness rose. For an instant he was too taken by surprise to speak. His silence added to Isobel's appalling conviction that she was going to drop dead or faint or do something equally beyond the bounds of common sense. She reflected that people often made up family differences over funerals.

'This is very kind of you,' said John Harkness. 'Won't you sit down? I hope you and Charles are both well.' John Harkness was worried. Charles must be ill or in trouble. Nothing less than a major calamity would have brought this unfriendly young woman to his house.

Isobel sought wildly for a remark. She had no idea whether the day was warm or cold. In view of her ignorance either comment seemed foolish. She said nothing.

John Harkness looked at her curiously. 'You are ill?' he said with concern. 'Is anything wrong?'

Isobel shook her head and abandoned the effort of finding a suitable opening. 'No, I'm not ill ... I'm frightened of you.'

The man started. 'God bless my soul! You are a strange girl.'

'I'm not a bit strange,' said Isobel. 'I think it was being in the mill.'

John Harkness could hardly be expected to follow the argument. He smiled. 'As a matter of fact, now that you mention it, I believe I am rather nervous of *you*.'

Isobel felt the strained atmosphere slipping away. 'You *are* like Charles,' she said in surprise.

'I presume that is intended as a great compliment?' said John Harkness.

The girl shook her head. 'I wasn't thinking of it like that. But when I got to know Charles first we used to become involved in the queerest conversations. He always said just the right thing. It must be a kind of gift. I nearly always say the wrong thing.'

'Your own father was rather given to the same habit,' said John Harkness. 'But he was none the worse for that. I liked your father very much.'

'And I like your son very much,' said Isobel.

They both laughed.

'I seem to have said the wrong thing again,' said Isobel.

'Not at all. Now at least we have a definite basis for future conversations, as the Foreign Secretaries have it.'

'I don't think I have much faith in Foreign Secretaries,' said Isobel. 'They are so diplomatic they never mention the subject they want to discuss. It seems a terrible waste of time.'

'And what do you want to discuss?' asked John Harkness.

'Well ... I ...' Isobel broke off. She wished that she had been less severe on Foreign Secretaries.

'Come,' said John Harkness, 'don't try to be tactful now. You must live up to your self-imposed reputation.'

'I want Charles to come back to Ringawoody.'

'I see,' said John Harkness. 'And what has Charles to say?'

'I haven't asked him. But I know he never wanted to go.'

'He left of his own free will,' John Harkness reminded her.

'No, he didn't. He had to resign ... after what you said.'

John Harness looked uncomfortable. 'When I first spoke to my son on the subject of his marriage I was unaware of certain aspects of the case which altered the position materially. Later I wished him to reconsider his decision, but he refused to do so and appeared unwilling to discuss the matter.'

Isobel sighed, not without impatience, but she wisely concluded that generalisations about the Harkness family and their common failings were not indicated at the moment – certainly not in the interests of a peaceful settlement. 'I think I was largely responsible for his neglecting to come to an agreement at that time,' she said. 'I did not realise that Charles could not be really contented away from Ringawoody. I was foolish and imaginative, and it seemed to me that if you disapproved of me so much ... you would ultimately turn Charles against me.'

'My dear child, what a remarkable idea! Even had I disapproved of you, which is certainly not the case, I would not dream of trying to influence Charles against his own wife, and you ought to know Charles well enough to see that any such influence would not weigh with him in the slightest.'

Isobel nodded. 'I know that, but you always seemed to be so powerful in Ringawoody. Everything had to be done the way you said. I did not think of you ever as making the best of a bad job.'

John Harkness smiled. He was not displeased. 'I'm afraid I have very little patience with bad jobs. However, I assure you, that at worst I did not look upon you as a hopelessly bad job. I was, and am, exceedingly sorry if any words or actions of mine hurt or offended you; and whatever Charles may or may not decide to do, I should like to think that you bear me no ill-will on that account.'

Isobel looked at the fire. 'I have not felt any ill-will towards you since I knew of your action in connection with my uncle's farm,' she brought out with difficulty.

John Harkness's face clouded. 'But you would not permit me to do a kindness to the memory of my old friend?'

'As things were ... or as I imagined they were, I could not accept a kindness from you, Mr Harkness,' she said.

'Yet you expect me to accept a kindness from you?' said John Harkness surprisingly.

Isobel coloured. This was the Charles element again. 'Yes,' she said frankly. 'I do, and I am glad that you realise that I am trying to do you a kindness. I hated coming here. You could not possibly imagine how much I did hate it. I knew very little about you, and what I thought I knew was not encouraging. I had no idea what attitude you might take or what you would say to me ... and I was quite definitely afraid. Charles once lectured me about pride. I knew at the time that what he said was true. But he's far worse himself.'

'You must be very sure that Charles wishes to return?' said John Harkness gruffly.

'I am quite sure,' replied Isobel, 'and I am also quite sure that you want him back.'

John Harkness hesitated, then with characteristic justice he remembered that this girl had risked rebuff, a risk of considerable significance to anyone familiar with the Martin breed. Though he failed to understand or sympathise with the nervous dread that had constituted the most trying part of Isobel's ordeal, he had every understanding and admiration for unselfishness real enough to abandon personal vanity in the interests of others.

'I shall not readily forget your action today,' he said at length. 'I need hardly say that nothing would give me greater pleasure than that my son should see his way to return to Ringawoody. I shall write and ask him to do so. Perhaps you will use your influence, which I am sure is very great, to persuade him that he is needed here – very badly.'

Charles did not need much persuasion from Isobel to obey his father's somewhat dictatorial communication. When Charles showed her the letter, Isobel was afraid that she might have a little trouble in making him see reason. John Harkness's method of expressing himself to his son, and his method of expressing himself to his daughter-in-law were two very different things. Charles, however, took no exception to his father's tone.

He returned, as he had left, with little explanation and no apology, in the orthodox Harkness manner. A few people noticed that the Head of the Firm, after a period of comparative mildness, had once more returned to his old domineering ways. If they grumbled a little they nevertheless accepted the affliction with fortitude. One could not expect a permanent change in a man like John Harkness. He liked things done in his own way.

Ringawoody clacked on monotonously indifferent to family quarrels or reconciliations. Managers might come and go; the mill preserved the legend of permanency. Shrill and persistent on dark, dank winter mornings the hooter sounded its call to labour. Heavy-shod feet clattered down the narrow street and up the Mill Wynd in obedience to the imperious command of the bleak, grey pile towering over the village. Ringawoody went on spinning yarn for the gleaming white webs of linen – Ulster's proudly cherished industry.

John Harkness was well satisfied, though, naturally, there were many occasions when he and his son failed to see eye to eye on matters even outside the immediate scope of mill routine. An interesting example was the argument which arose after the birth of Charles's first son. As far as John Harkness was concerned, there was no argument.

'I have decided to have him christened John,' he stated.

'I was thinking of advising Ferdinand,' said Charles. 'Don't you think it sounds well with Isobel?'

'When I require your advice, Charles,' said his father, 'I am still quite capable of asking for it.'

THE END

PATRICIA O'CONNOR

Patricia O'Connor/Norah Ingram with her husband Reg, July 1948
courtesy of Valerie Ingram

Patricia O'Connor (1905–83) was born in Co. Donegal, as Henrietta Norah O'Connor, and became Norah Ingram after her 1933 marriage. From 1937 she adopted 'Patricia O'Connor' as her professional name. Although starting her career as a novelist, she rose to prominence as a playwright, becoming one of the most staged Irish writers of the 1940s and 1950s. While frequently praised for her 'subtle character drawing', O'Connor was best known for her ability to skewer the shibboleths of Irish life. Such plays as *The Farmer Wants a Wife* (1955), which harshly viewed the traditions of farming life, proved extremely popular throughout Ireland for the wit and creativity of their plots. She worked as a teacher and lived most of her adult life in Co. Down.

NOVELS
The Mill in the North (Dublin, Talbot Press, June 1938)
Mary Doherty (London, Sands, December 1938)

PLAYS
all premiered by the Ulster Group Theatre
Highly Efficient (1942)
Voice out of Rama (1944)
Select Vestry (1945)
Master Adams (1949)
The Farmer Wants a Wife (1955)
Who Saw Her Die? (1956)
The Sparrow Falls (1959)